C A U S

(AN AVERY BL BOOK 2)

B L A K E   P I E R C E

Copyright © 2016 by Blake Pierce. All rights reserved. Except as permitted under the U.S. Copyright Act of 1976, no part of this publication may be reproduced, distributed or transmitted in any form or by any means, or stored in a database or retrieval system, without the prior permission of the author. This ebook is licensed for your personal enjoyment only. This ebook may not be re-sold or given away to other people. If you would like to share this book with another person, please purchase an additional copy for each recipient. If you're reading this book and did not purchase it, or it was not purchased for your use only, then please return it and purchase your own copy. Thank you for respecting the hard work of this author. This is a work of fiction. Names, characters, businesses, organizations, places, events, and incidents either are the product of the author's imagination or are used fictionally. Any resemblance to actual persons, living or dead, is entirely coincidental. Jacket image Copyright miljko, used under license from iStock.com.
ISBN: 978-1-63291-840-6

BOOKS BY BLAKE PIERCE

PROLOGUE

He lay hidden in the shadows of a parking lot fence and stared up at the three-story brick apartment building across the street. He imagined it was dinnertime for some, an hour where families would gather and laugh and share stories of the day.

Stories. He scoffed. Stories were for the weak.

The whistling shattered his silence. *Her* whistling. Henrietta Venemeer whistled as she walked. *So happy,* he thought. *So oblivious.*

His anger increased at the sight of her, a red, burning rage that bloomed in his entire visual landscape. He closed his eyes and took in a few deep breaths to make it stop. Drugs used to help with his anger. They had calmed him down and kept his mind light and carefree, but lately, even his prescriptions had failed. He needed something bigger to help balance in life.

Something cosmic.

You know what you have to do, he reminded himself.

She was a slight, older woman with a shock of red hair and a can-do attitude that permeated her every movement: hips swayed like she was dancing to an inner song and there was a noticeable hop in her step. She carried a bag of groceries and headed directly toward the brick building in a forgotten part of East Boston.

Go now, he commanded.

As she reached her building door and was fumbling for her keys, he left his spot and ambled across the street.

She opened her building door and entered.

Before the door shut, he placed his foot inside the opening. The camera that watched the foyer had been disabled earlier; he'd applied a film of clear spray-gel over the lens to obscure any images and yet give the illusion that the camera appeared in working order. The second foyer door had been disabled, too, its lock easy enough to break.

A whistle was still on her lips as she disappeared up a flight of stairs. He walked into the building to follow, giving no thought to the people on the street or other cameras that might have been watching from other buildings. Everything had been investigated earlier, and the timing of his attack had been aligned with the universe.

By the time she reached the third floor to unlock her front door, he was behind her. The door opened and as she walked into her apartment he grabbed her by the chin and clamped her mouth shut with his palm, stifling her screams.

Then he stepped inside and closed the door behind him.

CHAPTER ONE

Avery Black drove her flashy new ride, a black four-door Ford undercover cop car she'd bought, off the lot, and she smiled to herself. The smell of the new car and the feel of the wheel beneath her hands gave her a sense of joy, of starting anew. The old, white BMW that she'd bought as a lawyer, which had constantly reminded her of her previous life, was finally gone.

Yay, she inwardly cheered, as she did almost every time she sat behind the wheel. Not only did her new ride have tinted windows, black rims, and leather seats, but it came fully equipped with shotgun holster, computer frame on the dash, and police lights in the grilles, windows, and rearview mirrors. Better yet, when the blue-and-reds were turned off, it looked like any other vehicle on the road.

The envy of cops everywhere, she thought.

She'd picked up her partner, Dan Ramirez, at eight o'clock sharp. As always, he looked the model of perfect: slicked-back black hair, tan skin, dark eyes, decked out in the finest clothes. A canary yellow shirt was under a crimson jacket. He wore crimson slacks, a light-brown belt, and light-brown shoes.

"We should really do something tonight," he said. "Last night of our shift. Might be a Wednesday but it feels like a Friday."

He offered a warm smile.

In return, Avery batted her ice-blue eyes and flashed him a quick and loving grin, but then her features turned unreadable. She focused on the road and inwardly wondered what she was going to do about her relationship with Dan Ramirez.

The term "relationship" wasn't even accurate.

Ever since she'd taken down Edwin Peet, one of the strangest serial killers in recent Boston history, her partner had made his feelings known, and Avery had, in turn, let him know that she might be interested as well. The situation hadn't escalated much further. They'd had dinner, shared loving looks, held hands.

But Avery was worried about Ramirez. Yes, he was handsome and respectful. He'd saved her life after the Edwin Peet debacle and practically remained by her side the entire time during her recovery. Still, he was her partner. They were around each other five days a week or more, from eight AM to six or seven or later depending on a case. And Avery hadn't been in a relationship in years. The one time they kissed, it had felt like she was kissing her ex-husband, Jack, and she'd immediately pulled away.

3

She checked the dashboard clock.

They hadn't been in the car for five minutes and Ramirez was already talking about dinner. *You have to talk to him about this,* she realized. *Ugh.*

As they headed toward the office, Avery listened to the police band radio, as she did every morning. Ramirez suddenly turned on a jazz station, and they drove a few blocks listening to light jazz mixed with a police operator detailing various activities around Boston.

"Seriously?" Avery asked.

"What?"

"How am I supposed to enjoy the music *and* listen to the calls? It's confusing. Why do we have to listen to both at the same time?"

"All right, fine," he said in mock disappointment, "but I'd better get to listen to my music at some point today. It makes me feel calm and smooth, you know?"

No, Avery thought, *I don't know.*

She hated jazz.

Thankfully, a call came on the radio and saved her.

"We have a ten-sixteen, ten-thirty-two in progress on East Fourth Street off Broadway," said a scratchy female voice. "No shots have been fired. Any cars in the vicinity?"

"Domestic abuse," Ramirez said, "guy's got a gun."

"We're close," Avery replied.

"Let's take it."

She turned the car around, hit the lights, and picked up her transreceiver.

"This is Detective Black," she said and offered her badge number. "We're approximately three minutes away. We'll take the call."

"Thank you, Detective Black," the woman replied before she gave out the address, apartment number, and background information.

One of the many aspects Avery loved about Boston were the houses, small homes, most of them two to three stories high with a uniform structure that gave much of the city its communal feel. She hung a left onto Fourth Street and cruised to their destination.

"This doesn't mean we're off the hook on paperwork," she insisted.

"Nah, of course not." Ramirez shrugged.

The tone of his voice, however, coupled with his attitude and the unruly piles on his own desk, made Avery wonder if an early-morning drive had been the best decision.

4

Not much detective work was needed to discover the house in question. One police cruiser, along with a small crowd of people that were all hidden behind something, surrounded a blue stucco house with blue shutters and a black roof.

A Latino man stood on the front lawn in his boxers and a tank top. In one hand, he held the hair of a woman who was on her knees and crying. In his other hand, he simultaneously waved a gun at the crowd, the police, and the woman.

"*Get the fuck back!*" he yelled. "Every one of you. I see you there." He pointed his pistol toward a parked car. "Get the fuck away from that car! Stop crying!" he screamed at the woman. "You keep crying, I'm going to blow your head off just for pissing me off."

Two officers were on either side of the lawn. One had his gun drawn. The other had a hand on his belt and a palm up.

"Sir, please drop your weapon."

The man aimed at the cop with the pointed pistol.

"What? You wanna go?" he said. "Then shoot me! Shoot me, motherfucker, and see what happens. Shit, I don't care. We'll *both* die."

"*Don't fire your weapon, Stan!*" the other officer shouted. "Everybody just stay calm. Nobody is going to get killed today. Please, sir, just—"

"Stop fucking talking to me!" the man howled. "Just leave me alone. This is *my* house. This is *my* wife. You cheating motherfucker," he simmered and shoved the muzzle of his gun into her cheek. "I should clean out that dirty fuckin' mouth of yours."

Avery turned off her sirens and sidled up to the curb.

"Another fucking cop!?" the man seethed. "You guys are like cockroaches. All right," he said in a calm, determined way. "Someone is going to die today. You're not taking me back to prison. So you can all either go home, or someone is going to die."

"Nobody is going to die," said the first cop, "please. *Stan! Put your gun down!*"

"No way," his partner called out.

"*God damn it, Stan!*"

"Stay here," Avery said to Ramirez.

"Fuck that!" he stated. "I'm your partner, Avery."

"All right then, but listen up," she said. "All we need now is two more cops turning this into a bloodbath. Stay calm and follow my lead."

"What lead?"

"Just follow me."

Avery hopped out of the car.

"Sir," she commanded to the drawn officer, "put your gun *down*."

"Who the fuck are you?" he said.

"Yeah, who the fuck are you?" the Latino aggressor demanded.

"Both of you step away from the area," Avery said to the two officers. "I'm Detective Avery Black from the A1. I'll handle this. You too," she called to Ramirez.

"You told me to follow your lead!" he yelled.

"This *is* my lead. Get back in the car. Everyone step away from this scene."

The drawn officer spit and shook his head.

"Fuckin' bureaucracy," he said. "What? Just because you're in a few papers you think you're super cop now or something? Well, you know what? I'd love to see how you handle this, super cop." With his eyes on the perpetrator, he raised his gun and walked backward until he was hidden behind a tree. "Take it away." His partner followed suit.

Once Ramirez was back in the car and the other officers were safely out of firing distance, Avery stepped forward.

The Latino man smiled.

"Look at that," he said and pointed his gun. "You're the serial killer cop, right? Way to go, Black. That guy was fucking crazy. You got him good. *Hey!*" he yelled at the woman on her knees. "Stop fuckin' squirming around. Can't you see I'm trying to have a conversation?"

"What did she do?" Avery asked.

"Fuckin' bitch fucked my best friend. That's what she did. Didn't you, bitch?"

"Damn," Avery said. "That's cold. She ever do anything like that before?"

"Yeah," he admitted. "I guess she cheated on her last man with *me*, but shit, I married the bitch! That's got to count for something, right?"

"Definitely," Avery agreed.

He was slight of frame, with a narrow face and missing teeth. He glanced at the growing audience, then looked up at Avery like a guilty child and whispered:

"This don't look good, right?"

"No," Avery answered. "It's not good. Next time, you might want to handle this in the privacy of your own home. And quietly," she said softly and stepped closer.

"Why you getting so close?" he wondered with a cocked brow.

Avery shrugged.

"It's my job," she said as if it were a distasteful chore. "The way I see it? You have two choices. One: You come in quietly. You already screwed up. Too loud, too public, too many witnesses. Worst-case scenario? She presses charges and you have to get a lawyer."

"She's not pressing no fucking charges," he said.

"*I won't, baby. I won't!*" she swore.

"If she *doesn't* press charges, then you're looking at aggravated assault, resisting arrest, and a few other minor infractions."

"Will I have to serve some time?"

"Have you been arrested before?"

"Yeah," he admitted. "Five-year stint for attempted manslaughter."

"What's your name?"

"Fernando Rodriguez."

"You still on parole, Fernando?"

"Nah, parole was up two weeks ago."

"OK." She thought for a moment. "Then you'll probably have to be behind bars until this gets worked out. Maybe a month or two?"

"*A month?!*"

"Or two," she reiterated. "Come on. Let's be honest. After five years? That's nothing. Next time? Keep it private."

She was right in front of him, close enough to disarm him and free the victim, but he was already calming down. Avery had seen people like him before when dealing with some of the Boston gangs, men who'd been beaten down for so long that the slightest infraction could make them snap. But ultimately, when given a chance to relax and take stock of their situation, their story was always the same: they just wanted to be comforted, helped, and made to feel like they weren't alone in the world.

"You used to be a lawyer, right?" the man said.

"Yeah." She shrugged. "But then I made a stupid mistake and my life turned to shit. Don't be like me," she warned. "Let's end this now."

"What about her?" He pointed at his wife.

"Why would you want to be with someone like her?" Avery asked.

"I love her."

Avery sucked in her lips and challenged him with a stare.

"Does this *look* like love?"

The question seemed to genuinely bother him. With a furrowed brow, he glanced from Avery to his wife and back to Avery again.

"No," he said and lowered his gun. "This ain't no way to love."

"I'll tell you what," Avery said. "Give me that gun and let these guys take you in quietly and I'll promise you something."

"What promise?"

"I promise I'll check in on you and ensure you get treated right. You don't look like a bad guy to me, Fernando Rodriguez. You just look like you've had a rough life."

"You don't know the half of it," he said.

"No," she agreed. "I don't."

She held out a hand.

He let go of his hostage and handed over the gun. Instantly, his wife scrambled across the lawn and ran to safety. The aggressive cop that had been prepared to open fire came forward with a snarling look of thinly veiled jealousy.

"I'll take it from here," he sneered.

Avery got in his face.

"Do me a favor," she whispered. "Stop acting like you're better than the people you arrest and treat him like a human being. It might help."

The cop blushed in anger and seemed ready to push past and destroy the tranquil vibe that Avery had created. Thankfully, the second officer reached the Latino man first and handled him with care. "I'm going to cuff you now," he said softly. "Don't worry. I'll make sure you get treated right. I have to read you your rights. Is that OK? You have the right to remain silent…"

Avery backed away.

The Latino aggressor glanced up. The two held each other's gaze for a moment. He offered a nod of thanks, and Avery responded with a nod of her own. "I meant what I said," she reiterated before she turned to leave.

Ramirez had a big smile on his face.

"Shit, Avery. That was hot."

The flirtation bothered Avery.

"Makes me sick when cops treat suspects like animals," she said and turned back to watch the arrest. "I bet half the shootings in Boston could be avoided with a little respect."

"Maybe if there was a female commissioner like you in charge," he joked.

"Maybe," she replied and seriously thought about the implications.

Her walkie-talkie went off.

8

Captain O'Malley's voice came over the static.

"Black," he said. "Black, where are you?"

She picked up.

"I'm here, Cap."

"Keep your phone turned on from now on," he said. "How many times do I have to tell you that? And get over to the Boston Harbor Marina off Marginal Street in East Boston. We have a situation here."

Avery frowned.

"Isn't East Boston A7 territory?" she asked.

"Forget about that," he said. "Drop whatever you're doing and get over here as fast as you can. We've got a murder."

CHAPTER TWO

Avery reached the Boston Harbor & Shipyard by the Callahan Tunnel, which connected the North End to East Boston. The marina was off Marginal Street, right along the water.

The place was crawling with police.

"Holy shit," Ramirez said. "What the hell happened here?"

Avery took it slow into the marina. Police cars were parked in a haphazard pattern, along with an ambulance. Crowds of people that wanted to use their boats on this bright morning ambled about, wondering what they were supposed to do.

She parked and they both got out and flashed their badges.

Beyond the main gate and building was an expansive dock. Two piers jutted out from the dock in a V shape. Most of the police had clustered around the close end of one dock.

In the distance stood Captain O'Malley, dressed in a dark suit and tie. He was in deep discussion with another man in full police uniform. By the double stripes on his chest, Avery guessed the other guy was captain of the A7, which handled all of East Boston.

"Look at this character." Ramirez pointed at the man in uniform. "Did he just come from a ceremony or something?"

Officers from the A7 gave them hard stares.

"What's the A1 doing here?"

"Go back to the North End," another shouted.

Wind whipped across Avery's face as she walked down the pier. The air was salty and balmy. She tightened her jacket around her waist so it wouldn't fly open. Ramirez was having a difficult time with the intense gusts, which kept messing up his perfectly combed hair.

Docks jutted out at perpendicular angles on one side of the pier, and each dock was filled with boats. Boats were also lined on the other side of the pier: motorboats, expensive sailing vessels, and tremendous yachts.

A separate dock formed a T shape with the end of the pier. A single mid-sized white yacht was anchored in the middle of it. O'Malley, the other captain, and two officers talked while a forensics team scoured the boat and took pictures.

O'Malley sported the same gruff look as always: dyed black hair cut short, and a face that looked like he might have been a boxer in a former life, scrunched and wrinkled. Eyes were squinted from the wind and he seemed upset.

"She's here now," he said. "Give her a shot."

The other captain had a regal, stately quality about him: graying hair, lean face, and an imperious glance below a furrowed brow. He stood much taller than O'Malley and appeared slightly befuddled that O'Malley, or anyone outside of his team, would encroach on his territory.

Avery nodded to everyone.

"What's up, Captain?"

"Is this a party or what?" Ramirez smiled.

"Wipe that smile off your face," the stately captain spit. "This is a crime scene, young man, and I expect you to treat it as such."

"Avery, Ramirez, this is Captain Holt of the A7. He was gracious enough to—"

"Gracious my ass!" he snapped. "I don't know what kind of show the mayor is running, but if he thinks he can just walk all over my division, he has another think coming. I respect you, O'Malley. We've known each other a long time, but this is unprecedented and you know it. How would you feel if I walked over to the A1 and started to bark orders?"

"No one is taking over anything," O'Malley said. "You think I like this? We have enough work on our own side. The mayor called both of us, didn't he? I had a whole different day planned, Will, so don't act like this is me trying to make a power play."

Avery and Ramirez shared a look.

"What's the situation?" Avery asked.

"Call came in this morning," Holt said and motioned to the yacht. "Woman found dead on that boat. She's been identified as a local bookseller. Owns a spiritual bookshop over on Sumner Street and has for the last fifteen years. No record on her. Nothing outwardly suspicious about her."

"Except for the way she was murdered." O'Malley took over. "Captain Holt here was having breakfast with the mayor when the call came in. The mayor decided he wanted to come down and see it for himself."

"The first thing he says is 'Why don't we get Avery Black on this case,'" Holt concluded with dagger-eyes at Avery.

O'Malley tried to ease the situation.

"That's not what you told me, Will. You said your guys came in, they didn't understand what they were looking at, and so the mayor *suggested* you ask someone who's had some experience in this kind of thing."

"Either way," Holt snarled and pompously lifted his chin.

"Go take a look," O'Malley said and pointed to the yacht. "See what you can find. If she comes up empty," he added to Holt, "we'll be on our way. Does that seem fair?"

Holt stomped off toward his two other detectives.

"Those two are from his homicide squad," O'Malley indicated. "Don't look at them. Don't talk to them. Don't ruffle any feathers. This is a very delicate political situation. Just keep your mouth shut and tell me what you see."

Ramirez practically gushed as they walked up to the large yacht.

"This is one sweet ride," he said. "Looks like a Sea Ray 58 Sedan Bridge. Double decker. Gives you shade up top, AC inside."

Avery was impressed.

"How do you know all that?" she asked.

"I like to fish." He shrugged. "Never fished on anything like this before, but a man can dream, right? I should take you out on my boat sometime."

Avery had never truly enjoyed the sea. Beaches, sometimes; lakes, absolutely; but sailboats and motor vessels far out on the ocean? Panic attacks. She'd been born and raised on flat land, and the thought of being out on the bobbing, crashing tides, with no idea what might be lurking just beneath the waves, made her mind go to dark places.

As Avery and Ramirez passed by and prepared to board the boat, Holt and his two detectives ignored them. A photographer at the bow snapped one last picture and signaled to Holt. He made his way along the gunwale on the starboard side and wiggled his eyebrows at Avery. "You'll never look at a yacht the same way again," he joked.

A silver stepladder led to the ship's side. Avery climbed up, placed her palms on the black windows, and shimmied toward the front.

A middle-aged, saintly looking woman with wild red hair had been positioned on the front of the ship, just before the bow sidelights. She lay scrunched up on her side, facing east, with her hands gripped to her knees and her head down. If she'd been sitting upright she might have appeared asleep. She was completely naked, and the only visible wound was the dark line around her neck. *He snapped it,* Avery thought.

What made the victim stand out, beyond the nudity and the public display of her death, was the shadow she cast. The sun was up in the east. Her body was slightly angled upward, and it produced a mirror image of her scrunched form in a long, warped shadow.

"Fuck *me*," Ramirez whispered.

As Avery did when she was cleaning surfaces in her home, she got down low and glanced at the ship's bow. The shadow was either a coincidence or a meaningful sign by the killer, and if he'd left one sign, he might have left another. She moved from one side of the ship to the other.

In the glare of the sun, on the white surface of the ship's bow, right above the woman's head, between her body and her shadow, Avery spotted a star. Someone had used their finger to draw a star, either in spit or saltwater.

Ramirez called down to O'Malley.

"What did forensics say?"

"Found some hairs on the body. Could be from a carpet. The other team is still over at the apartment."

"What apartment?"

"The woman's apartment," O'Malley called up. "We believe she was abducted from there. No prints anywhere. Guy might have been wearing gloves. How he transferred her here, to a very visible dock, without anyone seeing, we don't know. He blacked out some of the marina cameras here. Must have been done right before the murder. She was possibly killed last night. Body seems unmolested, but the coroner has to give the final say."

Holt scoffed at nothing.

"This is a waste of our time," he snapped at O'Malley. "What can that woman possibly offer that my men haven't already discovered? I don't care about her last case *or* her public persona. As far as I'm concerned she's just a washed-up attorney who got lucky on her first major case because a serial killer, *that she defended in court, helped her*!"

Avery stood up, leaned on the railing, and observed Holt, O'Malley, and the two other detectives on the dock. Wind ruffled her jacket and pants.

"Did you see the star?" she asked.

"What star?" Holt called up.

"Her body is angled to the side and up. In the sunlight, it creates a shadow image of her form. Very distinct. Almost looks like two people, back-to-back. Between her body and that shadow, someone drew a star. Could be a coincidence, but the placement is perfect. Maybe we can get lucky if the killer drew it in spit."

Holt consulted with one of his men.

"Did you see a star?"

"No sir," replied a lean, blond detective with brown eyes.

"Forensics?"

The detective shook his head.

"Ridiculous," Holt mumbled. "A drawn star? A child could have done that. A shadow? Shadows are created by light. There's nothing special about that, Detective Black."

"Who owns the yacht?" Avery asked.

"A dead end." O'Malley shrugged. "Bigshot real estate developer. He's away in Brazil on business. Been gone for the last month."

"If the boat's been cleaned in the last month," Avery said, "then that star was put there by the killer, and since it's in perfect placement between the body and the shadow, it has to mean something. I'm not sure what, but something."

O'Malley glanced at Holt.

Holt sighed.

"Simms," he noted to the blond officer, "get forensics back here. See about that star, *and* the shadow. I'll call you when we're finished."

Miserably, Holt glanced at Avery, then finally, he shook his head.

"Let her see the apartment."

CHAPTER THREE

Avery walked slowly down the hall of the dim apartment building, flanked by Ramirez, her heart pounding with anticipation as it always did when entering a crime scene. At this moment, she wished she was anywhere but here.

She snapped out of it. She put her game face on and forced herself to observe every detail, however minute.

The victim's apartment door was open. An officer stationed outside moved away and allowed Avery and the others to duck under the crime scene tape and enter.

A narrow hallway led to a living room. A kitchen branched off from the hall. Nothing appeared out of the ordinary anywhere; just someone's very nice apartment. Walls were painted a light gray. There were bookshelves everywhere. Piles of books were stacked on the ground. Plants hung from the windows. A green couch faced a television set. In the only bedroom, the bed was made and topped with a lacy white blanket.

The only obvious disturbance to the apartment was in the living room, where a central rug was clearly missing. A dusty outline, along with a darker space, had been marked with numerous yellow police tags.

"What did forensics find here?" Avery asked.

"Nothing," O'Malley said. "No prints. No camera shots. We're in the dark right now."

"Anything taken from the apartment?"

"Not that we know. Change jar is full. Her clothes were neatly placed in her hamper. Money and ID were still in the pockets."

Avery took her time in the apartment.

As was her habit, she moved in small sections and observed every section thoroughly—the walls, the floors and wooden floorboards, any trinkets on shelves. A picture of the victim with two female friends stood out. She made a mental note to learn their names and contact each one. The bookshelves and piles were analyzed. There were stacks of female romance novels. The rest were mostly on spiritual subjects: self-help, religion.

Religion, Avery thought.

The victim had a star above her head.

Star of David?

Having observed the dead body on the boat and the apartment, Avery began to form a picture of the killer in her mind. He would have attacked from the hall. The kill was quick and he left no marks, made no mistakes. The victim's clothing and effects had

15

been left behind in a neat spot, so as not to disturb the apartment. Only the rug was moved, and it was dusty in that area and around the edges. Something about that harked to anger in the killer. *If he was so meticulous in every other way,* Avery wondered, *why not clean the dust from the rug sides? Why take the rug at all? Why not leave everything in perfect condition?* She worked it through: He snapped her neck, undressed her, put the clothing away and left everything in order, but then he rolled her in a rug and carried her out like a savage.

She headed over to the window and stared down at the street. There were a few places where someone could hide and observe the apartment without being noticed. One spot in particular called to her: a dark, narrow alleyway behind a fence. *Were you there?* she asked herself. *Watching? Waiting for the right moment?*

"Well?" O'Malley said. "What do you think?"

"We have a serial killer on our hands."

CHAPTER FOUR

"The killer is male, and strong," Avery went on. "He obviously overwhelmed the victim and had to carry her to the dock. Seems like a personal vendetta."

"How do you know that?" Holt asked.

"Why go through so much trouble with a random victim? Nothing appears to be stolen so it's not a robbery. He was precise about everything except that rug. If you spend so much time planning a murder, undressing the victim and putting her clothes in a hamper, why take *any* of her items? Seems like a planned gesture. He wanted to take *something*. Maybe to show he was powerful? That he could? I don't know. And leaving her on a boat? Naked and in full view of the harbor? This guy wants to be seen. He wants everyone to know he made this kill. You might have another serial killer on your hands. Whatever decision you're going to make about who handles this case," and she glanced at O'Malley, "you might want to make it quick."

O'Malley turned to Holt.

"Will?"

"You know how I feel about this," Holt sneered.

"But you'll go with the call?"

"It's a mistake."

"*But?*"

"Whatever the mayor wants."

O'Malley turned to Avery.

"Are you up for this?" he asked. "Be honest with me. You just came off a very high-profile serial murder. The press crucified you every step of the way. Once again, all eyes will be on you, but this time, the mayor is paying special attention. He asked for you specifically."

Avery's heart beat faster. Making a difference as a police officer was what she truly loved about her job, but catching serial killers and avenging the dead was what she craved.

"We have a lot of other open cases," she said. "And a trial."

"I can give everything to Thompson and Jones. You can oversee their work. If you take this on, this is priority number one."

Avery turned to Ramirez.

"You in?"

"I'm in." He nodded in earnest.

"We'll do it," she said.

"Good." O'Malley sighed. "You're on the case. Captain Holt and his men will deal with the body and the apartment. You'll have full access to the files and their full cooperation throughout this investigation. Will, who should they go to if they need information?"

"Detective Simms," he said.

"Simms is the lead detective you saw this morning," O'Malley relayed, "blond hair, dark eyes, tough all over. The boat and apartment are all being handled by the A7. Simms will contact you directly with any leads on this end. Maybe you should talk with the family for now. See what you can uncover. If you're right, and this is personal, they may be involved or have some information that can help."

"We're on it," Avery said.

*

A quick call to Detective Simms and Avery learned that the victim's parents lived just a bit further north, outside of Boston in the town of Chelsea.

Breaking the news to families was Avery's second-most loathed part of the job. Although she had a way with people, there was a moment, right after they learned about a death of a loved one, that complex emotions took hold. Psychiatrists called it the five stages of grieving, but Avery thought of it as slow torture. First, there was denial. Friends and relatives wanted to know everything about the body—information that would only make them grieve more, and no matter how much Avery offered, it was always impossible for the loved ones to imagine. Second came anger: at the police, at the world, at everyone. Bargaining came next. "Are you sure they're dead? Maybe they're still alive." These stages could happen all at once, or they could take years, or both. The last two stages usually happened when Avery was somewhere else: depression and acceptance.

"I have to say," Ramirez mused, "I don't like finding dead bodies, but this does free us up to work on this case. No more trial and no more paperwork. Feels good, right? We get to do what we want to do and not have to be bogged down in red tape."

He leaned over to kiss her cheek.

Avery pulled away.

"Not now," she said.

"No problem," he replied with his hands up. "I just thought, you know...that we were a thing now."

18

"Look," she said and had to really think about her next words. "I like you. I really do, but this is all happening too fast."

"Too fast?" he complained. "We've only kissed once in two months!"

"That's not what I mean," she said. "Sorry. What I'm trying to say is, I don't know if I'm ready for a full-blown relationship. We're partners. We see each other every week. I love all the flirtation and seeing you in the morning. I just don't know if I'm ready to move further."

"Whoa," he said.

"Dan—"

"No, no." He raised a hand. "It's OK. Really. I think I expected that."

"I'm not saying I want this to end," Avery reassured him.

"What *is* this?" he asked. "I mean, I don't even know! When we're working, you're all business, and when I try to see you after work, it's almost impossible. You were more loving towards me when you were in the hospital than in real life."

"That's not true," she said, but a part of her realized he was right.

"I like you, Avery," he said. "I like you a lot. If you need time, I'm OK with that. I just want to make sure you actually have some feelings for me. Because if you don't, I don't want to waste your time, or mine."

"I do," she said and glanced at him for a quick second. "Really."

"OK," he said. "Cool."

Avery kept driving, focusing on the road and on the changing neighborhood, forcing herself to snap back into work mode.

Henrietta Venemeer's parents lived in an apartment complex just past the cemetery on Central Avenue. From Detective Simms, Avery had learned they were both retired and would most likely be found at home. She hadn't called in advance. A hard lesson she'd learned early on was that a warning call could alert a possible killer.

At the building, Avery parked and they both walked up to the front door.

Ramirez rang the buzzer.

A long pause ensued before an elderly female answered.

"Yes? Who is it?"

"Mrs. Venemeer, this is Detective Ramirez with the A1 police division. I'm here with my partner, Detective Black. Can we please come up and speak with you?"

"*Who?*"

Avery leaned forward.

"*Police*," she snapped. "Please unlock the front door."

The door buzzed open.

Avery smiled at Ramirez.

"*That's* how you do it," she said.

"You never cease to amaze me, Detective Black."

The Venemeers lived on the fifth floor. By the time Avery and Ramirez exited the elevator, they could see an elderly woman peeking out from behind a locked door.

Avery took lead.

"Hi, Mrs. Venemeer," she said in her softest and clearest voice. "I'm Detective Black and this is my partner, Detective Ramirez." They both flashed their badges. "Can we come in?"

Mrs. Venemeer had a tangle of wiry hair just like her daughter, only hers was white. She wore thick black glasses and had on a white nightgown.

"What's this all about?" she worried.

"I think this would be easier if we could talk inside," Avery said.

"All right," she mumbled and let them in.

The entire apartment smelled like mothballs and old age. Ramirez made a face and jokingly waved at his nose the moment they entered. Avery hit him in the arm.

A television blared from the living room. On the couch was a large man that Avery assumed was Mr. Venemeer. He was dressed only in red boxers and a T-shirt that he probably wore to bed, and he seemed to have no awareness of them at all.

Oddly, Mrs. Venemeer sat down on the couch beside her husband, without any indication of where Avery or Ramirez might sit.

"What can I do for you?" she asked.

A game show played on the TV. The sound was loud. Every so often, the husband cheered from his seat, settled down, and mumbled to himself.

"Can you turn down the TV?" Ramirez asked.

"Oh no," she said. "John *has* to watch his *Wheel of Fortune*."

"This is about your daughter," Avery added. "We really need to talk to you, and we'd like your full attention."

"Honey," she said and touched her husband's arm. "These two officers want to talk about Henrietta."

He shrugged and growled.

Ramirez turned the television off.

"Hey!" John yelled. "What are you doing!? Turn that back on!"

20

He sounded drunk.

A bottle of half-filled bourbon was beside him.

Avery stood next to Ramirez and introduced them again.

"Hi," she said, "my name is Detective Black and this is my partner, Detective Ramirez. We have some very difficult news to share."

"I'll tell you what's difficult!" John snapped. "It's difficult dealing with a bunch of cops when I'm in the middle of my television program. Turn on that goddamn TV!" he snapped and tried to get out of his seat, but he couldn't seem to stand.

"Your daughter is dead," Ramirez said, and he squatted down to look him right in the eyes. "Do you understand? Your daughter is dead."

"What?" Mrs. Venemeer whispered.

"Henrietta?" John mumbled and sat back.

"I'm so sorry about this," Avery said.

"How?" the old woman mumbled. "I don't...*no*. Not Henrietta."

"Tell us what you're talking about!" John scoffed. "You can't come in here and say our daughter is dead. What the hell do you mean?!"

Ramirez took a seat.

Denial, Avery thought. *And anger.*

"She was found dead this morning," Ramirez said, "and identified because of her position within the community. We're not sure why it happened. Right now, we have a lot of questions. If you can, please just bear with us during this time and help answer some of them."

"*How?*" the mother cried. "How did it happen?"

Avery pulled a seat beside Ramirez.

"I'm afraid this is an ongoing investigation. We can't talk about any specifics at this time. Right now, we just need to know anything that *you* might know to help us identify her killer. Did Henrietta have a boyfriend? A close friend you might know about? Someone that might have had a grudge against her?"

"Are you sure it was *Henrietta*?" the mother wondered.

"Henrietta had no enemies!" John shouted. "Everybody loved her. A goddamn saint she was. Came over once a week with groceries. Helped out homeless people. This can't be right. This has got to be some kind of mistake."

Bargaining, Avery thought.

"I assure you," she said, "you'll both be called later this week to make a positive identification of the body. I know this is a lot to absorb. You've just received some terrible news, but please, let's stay focused on finding out who might have done this."

"No one!" John blared. "This is obviously a mistake. You have the wrong child. Henrietta had no enemies," he declared. "Was she hit by a bus? Did she fall off a bridge? At least give us *some* idea what we're dealing with here."

"She was killed," Avery offered. "That's all I can say."

"Killed," the mother whispered.

"Please," Ramirez said. "Anything you can think of? Anything at all. Even if it seems insignificant to you, it might be a big help to us."

"No," the mother replied. "She had no boyfriend. There's a circle of girlfriends she keeps. They were over last year for Thanksgiving. None of them could have done something like this. You must be wrong."

She looked up with pleading eyes.

"You must!"

CHAPTER FIVE

Avery parked at an empty spot on the street between police cruisers and braced herself as she looked over at the A7 police department headquarters on Paris Street in East Boston. Outside the station was a media circus. A news conference had been called to discuss the case and a number of television vans and cameras and reporters barred the way, despite numerous officers trying to get them to move.

"Your public awaits," Ramirez noted.

Ramirez seemed to want to be interviewed. His head was lifted high and he smiled at every reporter that turned his way. To his disappointment, none of them approached. Avery had her head down and walked as fast as possible to push her way into the station. She hated crowds. At one time in her life, when she was a lawyer, she'd loved when people knew her by name and flocked to her trials, but ever since she herself had been figuratively put on trial by the press, she'd learned to despise their attention.

Instantly, the reporters converged.

"Avery Black," one of them said with a mic in her face. "Can you please tell us anything about the woman murdered at the marina today?"

"Why are you on the case, Detective Black?" yelled another. "This is the A7. Were you transferred to this department?"

"How do you feel about the mayor's new Stop Crime campaign?"

"Are you and Howard Randall still an item?"

Howard Randall, she thought. Despite an overwhelming desire to cut all ties with Randall, Avery hadn't been able to get him out of her mind Every day since her last meeting with Randall, he'd found some way to creep into her thoughts. Sometimes, a simple smell or an image was all she needed to hear his words: "Does it bring back something from your childhood, Avery? What? Tell me..." Other times, while working on different cases, she tried to think like Randall would think to uncover the solution.

"Out of the way!" Ramirez yelled. "Come on! Make room. Let's go."

He put a hand on her back and led her into the station.

The A7 headquarters, a large brick and stone building, had recently received a major interior overhaul. Gone were the metal desks and typically sullen feel of a state-operated organization. In its place were sleek silver tables, colored chairs, and an open area for booking that looked more like the entrance to a playland.

Like the A1—only more modern—the conference room was encased in glass so that people could look out on the floor. A large, oval mahogany table was complete with microphones for each seat and a huge flat-screen TV for conferencing.

O'Malley was already seated at the table beside Holt. On either side of them were Detective Simms and his partner, and two people Avery guessed were the forensics specialist and the coroner. Two seats remained open at the bottom of the table near the entrance.

"Sit down," O'Malley waved. "Thanks for coming. Don't worry. I'm not going to be on your backs the entire time," he said to everyone, with special emphasis to Avery and Ramirez. "I just want to make sure we're all on the same page."

"You're always welcome here," Holt said with genuine affection toward O'Malley.

"Thanks, Will. Take it away."

Holt indicated his officer.

"Simms?" he said.

"All right," Simms said, "I guess I'm on. Why don't we start with forensics, then get the coroner's report, and then I'll tell you about the rest of our day," he said with emphasis to Captain Holt before he turned to the forensics specialist. "Sound good, Sammy?"

A lean Indian man was the head of their forensics team. He wore a suit and tie and gave a big thumbs-up when his name was mentioned.

"Yes sir, Mark," he practically gushed. "As we discussed, we have very little to go on. The apartment was clean. No blood, no sign of a struggle. The cameras were all disabled with a clear epoxy that you can buy at any hardware store. We found remnants of black glove fibers, but again, they offered no solid leads."

Detective Simms kept jerking his chin toward Avery. Sammy had trouble understanding who was in authority. He kept looking at Simms and Holt and everyone else. Eventually, he caught on and began to address Avery and Ramirez.

"We do, however, have something from the shipyard," Sammy said. "Obviously, the killer disabled the cameras there, in much the same way as the apartment. To get to the shipyard unnoticed would mean he had to work between eleven p.m., which is when the last worker left the marina, and six in the morning, when the first shifts came on. We found matching shoe prints in the shipyard and on the boat before the other police officers were on the scene. The foot is a ten and a half boot, of the Redwing variety. He seems to walk with a limp from a possible injury to his right leg, as the left shoe created a deeper indent than the right."

"Excellent," Simms said proudly.

"We checked into that drawn star on the bow as well," Sammy continued. "No genetic material could be found. However, we did find a black fiber within the star similar to the glove fibers in the apartment, so that was a very interesting connection, thank you for that, Detective Black." He nodded.

Avery nodded back.

Holt sniffed.

"Lastly," Sammy concluded, "we believe the body was carried to the shipyard in a rolled rug, as there were many rug fibers on the body and a missing rug from the house."

He nodded to indicate he was finished.

"Thanks, Sammy," Simms said. "Dana?"

A woman in a white lab coat, who looked like she would rather have been anywhere else but in that room, spoke next. She was middle-aged, with straight brown hair that came down to her shoulders, and a constant frown on her face.

"The victim died from a broken neck," she said. "There were bruises on her arms and legs that indicated she was hurled to the floor or against the wall. Body has probably been dead about twelve hours. There was no sign of forced entry."

She sat back with her arms folded.

Simms raised his brows and turned to Avery.

"Detective Black? Anything on the family?"

"That was a dead end," Avery said. "The victim saw her parents once a week to bring groceries and cook dinner. No boyfriend. No other close relatives in Boston. She does, however, have a close circle of friends that we'll have to speak with. The parents themselves aren't suspect. They could barely get off the couch. We would have begun researching the friends, but I wasn't sure about protocol," she said with a look to O'Malley.

"Thanks for that," Simms said. "Understood. I think after this meeting, you'll be in charge, Detective Black, but that's not my call. Let me tell you what *my* team discovered so far. We checked her phone records and email addresses. Nothing unusual there. Cameras in the building were disabled and no other lenses had sight on the building itself. However, we did find something at Venemeer's bookstore. It was open today. She has two full-time workers. They were unaware of the victim's death and genuinely shocked. Neither of them seemed like viable suspects, but both of them mentioned that the store has recently come under fire from a

25

local gang known as the Chelsea Death Squad. The name comes from their main hangout on Chelsea Street. I spoke with our gang unit and learned they're a relatively new Latino gang loosely affiliated with a bunch of other cartels. Their leader is Juan Desoto."

Avery had heard of Desoto from her gang days during her rookie years. He might be a small player in a new squad, but he'd been a big-time enforcer for a number of established gangs throughout Boston for years.

Why would a mob hitman with his own squad want to kill a local bookstore owner and then deposit the body in high-profile fashion on a yacht? she wondered.

"Sounds like you've got a *great* lead," Holt gushed. "It's distressing that we have to hand the reins over to a department on the other side of the channel. Sadly, however, that's part of life. Isn't it, Captain O'Malley? Compromise, yes?" He smiled.

"That's right," O'Malley reluctantly answered.

Simms sat taller.

"Juan Desoto would definitely be my number one suspect. If this was *my* case," he stressed, "I'd try and visit with him first."

The slight jab bothered Avery.

Do I really need this? she thought. Although she was utterly intrigued by the case, the blurry boundary lines between who handled what bothered her. *Do I have to follow his lead? Is he my supervisor now? Or can I do what I want?*

O'Malley seemed to read her mind.

"I think we're finished here. Right, Will?" he said before speaking exclusively to Avery and Ramirez. "After this, you two are in charge unless you need to refer back to Detective Simms over information we've just covered. Copies of the files are being made for you right now. They'll be sent over to the A1. So," he sighed and stood up, "unless there are any other questions, get started. I have a department to run."

*

The tension at the A7 kept Avery on edge until they were out of the building, past the news reporters, and back in her car.

"That went well," Ramirez cheered. "You do realize what just happened in there?" he asked. "You were just handed the biggest case A7 has probably had in years, and all because you're *Avery Black*."

Avery wordlessly nodded.

26

Being in charge came with a high price tag. She was able to do things her own way, but if problems arose they were on her head alone. Besides, she had a feeling that it wasn't going to be the last time she heard from the A7. *Feels like I have two bosses now,* she inwardly groaned.

"What's our next move?" Ramirez asked.

"Let's clean the slate with A7 and visit Desoto. Not sure what we'll find, but if his gang was harassing a bookstore owner, I'd like to know why."

Ramirez whistled.

"How do you know where to find him?"

"Everyone knows where to find him. He owns a small coffee shop on Chelsea Street, right by the expressway and the park."

"You think he's our guy?"

"Killing is nothing new to Desoto." Avery shrugged. "Not sure if this crime scene fits his MO, but he might know something. He's a legend throughout Boston. From what I understand, he's done jobs for the blacks, Irish, Italians, Hispanics, you name it. When I was a rookie they called him the Ghost Killer. For years, no one even believed he existed. Gang Unit had him pegged for jobs as far as New York City. No one could prove a thing. He's owned that coffee shop for as long as I've heard his name."

"You ever meet him?"

"No."

"Know what he looks like?"

"Yeah," she said. "I saw a photo of him once. Light-skinned and really, really big. I think his teeth were sharpened too."

He turned to her and smiled, but beneath that smile she could sense the same panic and rush of adrenaline she was starting to feel herself. They were heading into the lion's den.

"This should be interesting," he said.

CHAPTER SIX

The corner coffee shop was on the northern side of the underpass to the East Boston Expressway. A one-story brick building with large windows and a simple sign, *Coffee Shop,* served as the location. The windows were blacked out.

Avery parked right near the door entrance and got out.

A darkening had come to the sky. Toward the southwest, she could see the sunset horizon of orange, red, and yellow. A grocery store was on the opposite corner. Residential homes filled the rest of the street. The area was quiet and unassuming.

"Let's do this," Ramirez said.

After a long day just following along and sitting in a meeting, Ramirez seemed pumped and ready for action. His eagerness worried Avery. *Gangs don't like jumpy cops invading their hood,* she thought. *Especially ones with no warrant who are only there on hearsay.*

"Easy," she said. "I'll ask the questions. No sudden moves. No attitude of any kind, OK? We're just here to ask questions and see if they can help."

"Sure." Ramirez frowned, and his body language said otherwise.

A jingle of a bell came as they entered the shop.

The tiny space held four cushioned red booths and a single counter where people could order coffee and other breakfast items throughout the day. There were barely fifteen items listed on the menu and few customers.

Two old, thin Latino men that might have been homeless drank coffee at one of the booths on the left. A younger gentleman wearing sunglasses and a black fedora was slouched in one of the booths and turned toward the door. He wore a black tank top. A gun was clearly holstered in a shoulder strap. Avery glanced at his shoes. *Eight and a half,* she thought. *Nine, tops.*

"*Puta,*" he whispered at the sight of Avery.

The older men seemed oblivious.

No chef or takeout employee was visible behind the counter.

"Hi there." Avery waved. "We'd like to speak to Juan Desoto if he's around."

The young man laughed.

Quick words were spoken in Spanish.

"He says, 'fuck you, cop whore and your bitch boy,'" Ramirez translated.

"Lovely," Avery said. "Listen, we don't want any trouble," she added and held up both palms in submission. "We just want to ask Desoto a few questions about a bookstore on Sumner Street that he doesn't seem to like."

The man sat up and pointed at the door.

"Get the fuck out, *cop!*"

There were a lot of ways Avery could have handled the situation. The man was carrying a gun and she guessed it was loaded and had no license. He also seemed ready to engage despite the fact that nothing had actually occurred. That, combined with the empty counter, led her to believe that something might be going on in a back room. *Drugs,* she guessed, *or they have some hapless store owner back there and are beating him to a pulp.*

"All we want is a few minutes with Desoto," she said.

"*Bitch!*" the man snapped and stood and pulled his gun.

Ramirez instantly drew.

The two older men continued to drink their coffee and sit in silence.

Ramirez called out over the barrel of his gun.

"Avery?"

"Everybody calm down," Avery said.

A man appeared in a cooking window behind the main counter, a big man by the look of his neck and round cheeks. He seemed to be leaning into the window, which gave him a foreshortened height. His face was partially hidden in dim shadow; a bald, light-skinned Latino with a humorous glint in his eyes. A smile was on his lips. In his mouth was a grill that made all of his teeth look like sharp diamonds. No outward display of malice could be observed, but he was so cool and calm given the tense situation that it made Avery wonder why.

"Desoto," she said.

"No weapons, no weapons," Desoto mentioned from the square window. "Tito," he called, "put your gun on the table. Cops. Put your guns on the table. No weapons here."

"No way," Ramirez said and kept his gun pointed at the other man.

Avery could feel the short blade she kept attached to her ankle, just in case she ran into trouble. Also, everyone knew they were headed to Desoto's place. *We'll be all right,* she thought. *I hope.*

"Put it down," she said.

As a show of good faith, Avery gently pulled her Glock out with her fingertips and put it on the table between the two older men.

29

"Do it," she said to Ramirez. "Put it on the table."

"Shit," Ramirez whispered. "This is no good. No good." Still, he complied; placed his gun on a table. The other man, Tito, then put his own gun down and smiled.

"Thank you," Desoto said. "Don't worry. No one wants your cop guns. They'll be safe right there. Come. Talk."

He disappeared from view.

Tito indicated a small red door, practically impossible to notice given its location behind one of the booths.

"You first," Ramirez said.

Tito bowed and entered.

Ramirez stepped through next and Avery followed.

The red door opened into the kitchen. A hallway moved further back. Directly in front of them were basement stairs, steep and dark. At the bottom was another door.

"I've got a bad feeling about this," Ramirez whispered.

"*Quiet,*" Avery whispered.

A poker game was being played in the room beyond. Five men, all Latino, well-dressed and strapped with guns, went silent on their approach. The table was packed with money and jewelry. Couches lined the walls of the large space. On numerous shelves, Avery noticed machine guns and machetes. One other door was visible. A quick glance at their feet revealed that none of them had shoes large enough to match the killer.

On the couch, arms splayed wide, and with a huge smile on his face that exposed the grill of razor teeth, sat Juan Desoto. His body was more bull than man, pumped up and chiseled from daily workouts and, Avery guessed, steroids. A giant even though seated, he might have stood to nearly seven feet tall. His feet, similarly, were huge. *At least a twelve,* Avery thought.

"Relax, everyone, relax," Desoto commanded. "Play, play," he urged his men. "Tito, get them something to drink. What would you like, Officer *Black,*" he said with emphasis.

"You know me?" Avery asked.

"I don't know you," he replied. "I know *of* you. You arrested my little cousin Valdez two years ago, and some of my good friends in the West Side Killers. Yes, I have many friends in other gangs," he said at Avery's surprised look. "Not all gangs fight each other like animals. I like to think *bigger* than that. Please. What can I get for you?"

"Nothing for me," Ramirez said.

"I'm fine," she added.

Desoto nodded to Tito, who left the way he'd come. All men at the table continued to play cards except one. The odd man out was a spitting image of Desoto, only much smaller and younger. He muttered something to Desoto and the two of them had a fiery conversation.

"That's Desoto's little brother," Ramirez translated. "He thinks they should just kill both of us and dump us in the river. Desoto is trying to tell him that that's why he's always in prison, because he thinks too much when he should just keep his mouth shut and listen."

"*Sientate!*" Desoto finally shouted.

Reluctantly, his little brother sat down but he glared hard at Avery.

Desoto took in a breath.

"You like being a big celebrity cop?" he asked.

"Not really," Avery said. "Gives guys like you a target in the police department. I don't like to be a target."

"True, true," he said.

"We're looking for information," Avery added. "A middle-aged woman named Henrietta Venemeer owns a bookstore on Sumner. Spiritual books, new age, psychology, things like that. Rumor has it you don't like the shop. She was being harassed."

"By *me*?" he noted in surprise and pointed to himself.

"By you or your men. We're not sure. That's why we're here."

"Why would you come all the way into the devil's den to ask about some woman at a bookshop? Please, explain this to me."

No recognition of Henrietta or the bookstore appeared on his face. In fact, Avery thought he was insulted by the accusation.

"She was murdered last night," Avery said and paid careful attention to the men in the room and how they reacted. "Her neck was broken and she was tied to a yacht at the marina on Marginal Street."

"Why would I do this?" he asked.

"That's what we want to find out."

Desoto began to speak to his men in very quick and agitated Spanish. His little brother and another man seemed genuinely annoyed that they would be accused of something so clearly beneath them. The other three, however, turned sheepish under the interrogation. An argument ensued. At one point, Desoto stood up in anger and displayed his full height and size.

"These three have been to the shop," Ramirez whispered. "They robbed it twice. Desoto is pissed because this is the first time he's hearing about it, and he never got his cut."

31

With a loud roar, Desoto hammered his fist onto the table and cracked it in half. Bills and change and jewelry went flying. A necklace nearly whipped into Avery's face and she was forced to stand back against the door. All five men pushed away in their chairs. Desoto's little brother yelled out in frustration and raised his arms. Desoto kept his fury squarely placed on one man in particular. A finger was pointed in the man's face, and a threat was given and received.

"That guy took the others to the shop," Ramirez whispered. "He's in trouble."

Desoto turned with his arms wide.

"I apologize," he said. "My men did indeed accost this woman in her shop. Twice. This is the first I've ever heard of it."

Avery's heart was beating fast. They were in an isolated room full of angry criminals with weapons, and regardless of Desoto's words and gestures, he was an intimidating presence, and, if the rumors were true, a mass murderer. Suddenly, the feel of her small blade so far out of reach wasn't as comforting as she'd thought.

"Thanks for that," Avery said. "Just to be sure we're on the same page, would any of your men have any reason to *kill* Henrietta Venemeer?"

"No one kills without my approval," he flatly stated.

"Venemeer was strangely placed on the ship," Avery pushed. "In full view of the harbor. A star was drawn above her head. Would that mean anything to you?"

"Do you remember my cousin?" Desoto asked. "Michael Cruz? Little guy? Skinny?"

"I don't."

"You broke his arm. I asked him how a little girl could have bested him, and he said that you were very fast, and very strong. Do you think you could take *me*, Officer Black?"

The downward spiral began.

Avery could feel it. Desoto was bored. He'd answered their questions and he was bored and angry and he had two unarmed cops in his private room beneath a shop. Even the men who'd been playing poker were fully locked onto both of them.

"No," she said. "I think you could murder me in hand-to-hand combat."

"I believe in an eye for an eye," Desoto said. "I believe when information is given, information should be received. *Balance*," he stressed, "is very important in life. I have given you information. You arrested my cousin. You have now taken from me twice. You see this, yes?" he asked. "You *owe* me something."

32

Avery backed up and assumed her traditional jujitsu stance, legs bent and slightly parted, arms up and hands open under her chin.

"What do I owe you?" she asked.

With only a grunt, Desoto jumped forward, cocked his right arm, and punched.

CHAPTER SEVEN

The room emptied in Avery's mind; it turned black, and all she could see were the five men, and feel Ramirez next to her, and see Desoto's fist moving closer to her face. She called it *the fog*, a place where she'd often been during her running days—another world, separate from her physical existence. Her jujitsu instructor had called it "the ultimate awareness," a place where focus became selective, so the senses were more heightened around specific targets.

She spun into Desoto's arm and gripped his wrist. At the same time, her hip popped back into his body for leverage, and she used his own momentum to throw him into the basement door. Wood cracked and the giant man crashed hard.

Without breaking her stride, Avery spun and kicked an attacker in the stomach. After that, everything moved in slow motion. Each of the five men was targeted for maximum damage with minimal aggression. A jab to the throat made one fall to the ground. A kick to the groin followed by a hard back-spin and another man crashed on the broken table. She lost Desoto's little brother for a second. She turned to see him about to punch her with a pair of brass knuckles; Ramirez jumped in and tackled him to the ground.

Desoto roared and grabbed Avery in a bear hug from behind.

The massive weight of his body was like a cement block. Avery couldn't break his hold. She kicked at the air. He lifted her up and threw her into a wall.

Avery slammed into a shelving system and the entire unit fell on her head when she dropped to the ground. Desoto kicked her in the stomach; the blow was so powerful it lifted her up. Another kick and her neck snapped back. Desoto lowered down. Thick arms clutched her neck in a dangerous choke. A quick lift and she was up—feet dangling.

"I could snap your neck," he whispered, "like a twig."

Groggy.

Her mind was groggy from the blows. Air was hard to take in.

Focus, she commanded. *Or you're dead.*

She tried to flip over his body, or break the hold with his arms. An iron grip held her fast. Something slammed into Desoto's back. He lowered Avery's feet to the ground and looked behind him to see Ramirez with a chair.

"That didn't hurt you?" Ramirez asked.

Desoto growled.

Avery collected herself, lifted her foot, and stomped her heel into his toes.

"*Ah!*" Desoto howled.

He wore a white button-down T-shirt, tan shorts, and flip-flops; Avery's heel had cracked two bones. Instinctively, he let go, and by the time he was ready to grip her again, Avery was in stance. One quick punch to his throat was followed by a jab to his solar plexus.

An iron bat was on the ground.

She picked it up and swatted him in the head.

Desoto instantly went limp.

Two of his men were already down, including the little brother. A third—who'd been watching her battle with Desoto—widened his eyes in surprise. He drew his gun. Avery swatted his hand with the bat, spun with the momentum, and clocked him in the face. He crashed into a wall unit.

The last two men had overtaken Ramirez.

Avery swung the bat into the back of one man's knees. He flipped up. She brought the steel down on his chest and kicked him hard in the face. The other man punched her in the jaw and followed with a screaming tackle onto the poker table.

They crashed down together.

The man was on top and rained down blows. Avery finally caught a wrist and rolled. He fell off and she was able to spin and trap his arm in a submission hold. Avery lay perpendicular to his body. Her legs were over his belly and his arm was straight and hyper-extended.

"Let go! Let go!" he cried out.

She lifted a leg and kicked him in the face until he passed out.

"*Fuck you!*" she yelled.

The room was silent. All five men, including Desoto, were out cold.

Ramirez groaned and got to his hands and knees.

"Jesus..." he whispered.

Avery spotted a gun on the floor. She grabbed it and pointed it at the basement door. No sooner had she aimed than Tito appeared.

"Don't you lift that gun!" Avery howled. "You hear me!? Don't you do it."

Tito glanced at the gun in his hand.

"You lift that gun and I shoot."

The scene in the room was impossible for Tito to believe; his mouth practically fell open when he saw Desoto.

"You do all this?" he asked seriously.

"Drop the gun!"

Tito aimed at her.

Avery fired two shots into his chest and sent him flying back into the staircase.

CHAPTER EIGHT

Outside the coffee shop, Avery held a bag of ice over her eye. Two nasty bruises were throbbing beneath it, and her cheek was swollen. It was also hard to breathe, which made her think she'd fractured a rib, and her neck was still sore and red from the tight squeeze of Desoto.

Despite the abuse, Avery felt good. *Better* than good. She'd successfully defended herself against a giant killer and five other men.

You did it, she thought.

She'd spent years learning to fight, countless years and hours when she was the only one in the dojo, just sparring with herself. She'd been in other fights before, but none against five men, and certainly none against someone as powerful as Desoto.

Ramirez sat on the curb. He'd been on the verge of collapse ever since the basement. Compared to Avery, he was in bad shape: face riddled with cuts and swollen spots and constant dizzy spells.

"You were an animal down there," he muttered. "An animal..."

"Thanks?" she said.

Desoto's diner was in the heart of A7, so Avery had felt obligated to call in Simms for backup. An ambulance was on the scene, along with numerous A7 cops to take Desoto and his men in for assault, weapons possession, and other small infractions. Tito's body—wrapped in a black bag—was brought up first and loaded into the back of the emergency vehicle.

Simms appeared and shook his head.

"It's a mess down there," he said. "Thanks for the extra paperwork."

"Would you have rather I called my own people?"

"No," he admitted, "I guess not. We've got three different departments all trying to pin something on Desoto, so at the very least this can help shake the tree. I don't know what you were thinking going into that place without backup, but nice work. How did you take all six of them on your own?"

"I had help," Avery said with a nod to Ramirez.

Ramirez raised a hand in acknowledgment.

"What about the yacht murder?" Simms asked. "Any connection?"

"I don't think so," she said. "Two of his men robbed the store twice. Desoto was surprised about it, and pissed. If the two other clerks corroborate the story, I think they're in the clear. They wanted money, not a dead store owner."

Another cop appeared and waved at Simms.

Simms gave a light tap on Avery's shoulder.

"You might want to get out of here," he said. "They're bringing them up now."

"No," Avery said. "I'd like to see him."

Desoto was so large he had to dip out of the front door. Two cops were on either side of him, and one was at his back. Compared to everyone else, he looked like a giant. His men were brought up behind him. All of them were led toward a police van. As he drew close to Avery, Desoto paused and turned; none of the cops could make him move.

"Black," he called.

"Yeah?" she said.

"You know that target you were talking about?"

"Yeah?"

"Click, click, *boom*," he said with a wink.

He stared at her for another second before he allowed police to load him in the van.

Idle threats were part of the job. Avery had learned that a long time ago, but someone like Desoto was the real thing. Outwardly, she stood her ground and stared back at him until he was gone, but on the inside, she was barely keeping it together.

"I need a drink," she said.

"No way," Ramirez muttered. "I feel like shit."

"I'll tell you what," she said. "Any bar you want. Your choice."

He instantly perked up.

"Really?"

Avery had never offered to go out to a bar that Ramirez wanted. When he went out, he drank with the squad, while Avery chose quiet, low-key bars around her own neighborhood. Ever since they'd been a sort-of item, Avery had never once accompanied him out, or had a drink with anyone else in the department.

Ramirez stood up too fast, swooned, and caught himself.

"I got just the place," he said.

CHAPTER NINE

"*Fuckin' A!*" Finley roared in a drunken stupor. "You just took out six members of the Chelsea Death Squad, including Juan Desoto? I don't believe it. *I don't fuckin' believe it.* Desoto is supposed to be a monster. Some people don't even believe he exists."

"She did it," Ramirez swore. "I was right there, man. I'm telling you, she did it. Girl is like a kung-fu master or something. You should have seen her. As fast as lightning. I'd never seen anything like it. How did you learn to fight like that?"

"A lot of hours in the gym," Avery said. "No life. No friends. Just me, a bag, and a lot of sweat and tears."

"You've got to teach me some of those moves," he pleaded.

"You were doing pretty well there yourself," Avery said. "You saved me twice, if I remember correctly."

"That's true. I did do that," he agreed so that everyone could hear.

They were in Joe's Pub on Canal Street, a cop bar only a few blocks away from the A1 police station. At the large wooden table was everyone who'd been on Avery's previous Homicide Squad: Finley, Ramirez, Thompson, and Jones, along with two other beat cops that were friends with Finley. Homicide supervisor for the A1, Dylan Connelly, was at another table not far away, having a drink with some men that worked in his unit. Every so often, he glanced up seemingly to catch Avery's eye; she never noticed.

Thompson was the largest person in the entire the bar. Practically albino, he had extremely light-colored skin, with fine blond hair, full lips, and light-colored eyes. A drunken gaze turned sour at Avery.

"*I* could take you," he declared.

"*I* could take her," Finley snapped. "She's a *girl*. Girls can't fight. Everyone knows that. This must have been a fluke. Desoto was sick and his men were all suddenly blinded by chick-beauty. No way she beats them cold. No way."

Jones, a lean, older Jamaican, leaned forward with incredible interest.

"How you take Desoto?" he wondered. "Seriously. No gym shit. I be in the gym too and look at me. I barely gain a pound."

"I got lucky," Avery said.

"Yeah, but, *how*?" he truly wanted to know.

"Jujitsu," she said. "I used to be a runner, back when I was in law, but after that whole scandal, jogging around the city wasn't really my thing anymore. I enrolled in a jujitsu class and spent hours there every day. I think I was trying to purge my soul or something. I liked it. A lot. So much so that the instructor gave me keys to the gym and said I could go whenever I wanted."

"Fuckin' *jujitsu*," Finley said like it was a bad word. "I don't need no karate. I just call my crew and they go *pop-pop-pop*!" he cried and pretended to fire a machine gun. "They'll blow everybody away!"

A round of shots were ordered to commemorate the event.

Avery played pool, threw darts, and by ten o'clock, she was hammered. This was the first time she'd ever actually hung out with her squad, and it gave her a true sense of community. In a rare, extremely vulnerable moment, she put her arm around the much shorter Finley at the pool table. "You're all right by me," she said.

Finley, seemingly bedazzled by her touch and the fact that a tall blond goddess stood next to him, was momentarily speechless.

Ramirez remained slumped over at the bar and sitting alone, where he'd been all night. A walk over nearly landed Avery face down on the floor. She put her arm around his neck and kissed him on the cheek.

"Does that feel better?" she asked.

"That hurt."

"Aw," she cooed. "Let's get out of here. I'll make it better."

"Nah," he mumbled.

"What's wrong?"

Ramirez was distraught when he turned around.

"*You*," he said. "You're incredible at everything you do. What am I? I feel like I'm your sidekick sometimes. You know? Until you came along, I thought I was a great cop, but whenever we're together I just see my flaws. This morning—who else could have stopped that guy from shooting that cop? At the dock, who else could have seen what you saw? Who else could have gotten Desoto to let you into his crib and then *beaten* Desoto? You're just so good, Avery, it makes me question my own value."

"Come on," Avery said and pushed her forehead into his. "You're a great cop. You saved my life. *Again*. Desoto would have cracked my neck in two."

"Anyone could have done that," he said and wiggled away.

"You're the best-dressed cop I know," she offered, "*and* the most enthusiastic cop, and you always make me smile with your positive attitude."

40

"Really?"

"Yeah," she pushed. "I get into my head too much. I could stay there for weeks. You force me out of my shell and make me feel like a woman."

She kissed him on the lips.

Ramirez lowered his head.

"Thanks for that," he said. "Really. Thanks. That means a lot. I'm OK. Just give me a minute, OK? Let me finish my drink and think about some things."

"Sure," she said.

The bar was even more packed than when they'd first arrived. Avery scanned the crowd. Thompson and Jones had left. Finley was playing pool. There were a couple of other officers she recognized from their office, but no one she particularly wanted to meet. Two well-dressed men waved her down and pointed at drinks. She shook her head.

Images flashed through her mind: Desoto's hands around her neck, and the woman on the boat with her eerie shadow and star.

Avery ordered another drink and found a quiet table near a back corner. To anyone watching, she knew she must have looked crazy: a lone woman with a beaten-up face, hands on the table around a drink, and eyes focused squarely at nothing while she inwardly combed through the events of the day to find connections.

Desoto, dead end.

Parents, dead end.

Friends? Avery realized she needed to follow up with them at some point, probably sooner rather than later.

Why did the killer draw a star? she wondered.

She thought about the apartment where the murder had taken place, the books, the clothing in a hamper, and the missing rug. He's big, she thought, and strong, and he's definitely got a chip on his shoulder. Cameras were disabled, which means he's also stealthy. Military training? Maybe.

She checked off another box.

Definitely personal, she mulled. Go back in Venemeer's past. Find out who else worked at the shop, or dated her in school. Compile a list. After you have your list, maybe talk with the parents again so they can verify.

Pieces began to form, pieces to a puzzle she had yet to complete.

Ramirez stood right in front of her, watching.

"Hey," Avery said and covered her face in embarrassment.

"Look at you." He smiled back. "What are you doing?"

A blush painted her cheeks.

"This is how I work," she said.

He sat down next to her.

"How?" he asked. "Tell me."

"I just...go through it in my mind," she said. "All the facts. All the pieces. Try to mentally look for connections. I create a checklist of leads to pursue so we don't let anything fall through the cracks. I have to be thorough."

"Why?" he asked. "Why are you so good at this?"

The image of her father came to her, shotgun in hand, the muzzle pointed at her face. "Stop crying or I'll give you something to cry about!"

Escape, she thought.

That was all Avery had wanted for most of her life: to escape from her past. But escape meant she had to have a plan, and plans always had a way of going awry.

"It was the only way out," she said.

"Out? Of what?"

Avery faced him, and shared a piece of information she hadn't said aloud in years.

"I was an orphan. Did you know that?"

Ramirez sat back in awe.

"No!" he cried. "I would have never pegged you as an orphan. I'm a *really* bad cop."

"Don't think that." She smiled and held his hand.

"Anyway," she went on, "I was a foster kid for about six years. I went through a lot of homes, was picked up by a few families. House mothers. That's what they're called. They get paid to take in young children with nowhere else to go. Everybody's happy. The state gets to wipe their hands clean of wayward children. Crappy people get to have slaves."

"Avery. I am *so* sorry."

"There was this one house mother—"

A newspaper was slapped down on the table.

Dylan Connelly stood above them.

"You seen this?" he said. "It's the late edition. All over the Internet. A copy of the letter was mailed to A7. O'Malley is waiting on us. Wants the entire team in to go over what you've discovered so far. It's from your killer."

The cover of the paper read: *Murder at Marina*, and showed a shot of the victim on the bow of a yacht docked to a pier. Lines from the article stood out: "Saliva swab on the letter matches that of the slain woman," and "Possible bookstore connection." Avery was mentioned twice by name: once as an investigator from the A1 brought in to help with the case, and once as a possible love interest of captured serial killer Howard Randall.

A smaller caption read: *Letter from the Murderer!* The picture displayed a zoom-in of words scrawled on paper.

Avery flipped to the page.

The letter was a full side. The killer's note was written like a poem:

How can you break the cycle?
How can you take advantage of each moment in life?
I have found the key.
I can unlock the prize.
Come all who dare.
I defy you.
The first body is set. More will come.

Avery set it down, her entire body trembling.
More will come.
She knew, with sudden certainty, that he was right.

CHAPTER TEN

Before Avery and Ramirez even walked into the A1 conference room, they could hear O'Malley screaming into the speakerphone.

"Completely unacceptable, Will! You were supposed to share everything with us. We're handling this case now. But instead, you received a huge piece of evidence and decided to keep it for yourself. When were you going to call us?"

"We just received the letter this afternoon," Holt blared back from the speaker.

"How did the papers get it?"

"They got a copy. We have the original here, but the killer made copies. The way I understand it, he sent them to *every* newspaper."

"No way the papers would know that splotch on the bottom of the letter was a saliva swab. That had to come from your department. So you got the letter, you had forensics check it out, you matched the saliva to the victim, and then you told someone. That's the only way this could have happened, Will. The first call you should have made was to Detective Black. Do you know where I am right now? I'm in the office. You know where I *should* be? I *should* be in bed with my wife. But instead, I'm here. That's because you didn't do your job, and now we have a publicity nightmare on our hands and the mayor is pissed."

"Calm down, Mike, calm down."

"I won't calm down until you tell me the truth!"

"The truth is, we had no idea that letter was connected to the victim we found this morning. It came in the regular mail, it was opened by one of our staff, and someone had the foresight to send it to forensics. It just so happened that there was a match."

"Who called the papers?"

"They must have called us."

"The leak definitely came from your department."

"I'll handle it."

"You'd *better* handle it, and next time, we expect a call."

He hung up.

"*Shit!*" he cried.

Dylan Connelly sat down.

"Captain, why don't you go home?" he said. "I can handle this."

"I can't go anywhere just yet," O'Malley replied, "because the mayor pulled me into his Everybody-Holds-Hands crime campaign and now I'm screwed. Don't worry. I'm going home soon. You're here to learn everything you can from Black and Ramirez and act as a liaison with Simms over at the A7 so this doesn't happen again. You two are friends, right?"

"We were in the academy together."

"Good. Once we're through here, call him up. If he doesn't want to talk to myself or Black, he's at least got to talk to you."

"It might not be his fault," Avery said. "He was a little busy earlier."

"Oh yeah," O'Malley snapped. "That reminds me. Nice face," he noted to Avery. "What the hell were you doing in the gang den of Juan Desoto?"

"It was a lead. We were following up."

"You were supposed to *talk* to him," O'Malley said. "Instead, the A7 has five guys in a holding cell and one in a hospital. How do we know they won't file charges?"

"It was clean, Captain," Ramirez said. "We went in—"

"Did I ask you?" O'Malley snapped. "No, I didn't. Not for nothing, Ramirez, but Black is the lead on this case and it was her call to go in. What happened?"

"We just wanted to talk. Desoto made it personal. Apparently, I beat up his cousin a few years back, but I don't remember it. Desoto swung first and tried to kill me—both of us," she corrected with a look at Ramirez. "If we didn't fight hard, we'd both be dead."

"Cross-departmental assignments," O'Malley spit. "Bullshit. Well, watch your back. Desoto won't take that lightly. No word yet, but I'd be looking over my shoulder for a while, and you should too. Now," he sighed. "Back to this letter. Holt and his team scanned it for prints. Nothing. Trying to track down pen ink is futile. We have a handwriting style, but until we get a suspect, it's useless. No one knows how the letter got into their mailbox. Guy must be a ghost. Any ideas? Anyone?" he said with a glance at Ramirez. "I guarantee you, the A7 is going to try and crack this case just to prove they didn't need our help."

A copy of the letter was on the table. Avery leaned over to scrutinize every line.

"'Break the cycle,'" she read, "'take advantage of each moment.' The victim ran a spiritual bookstore. Self-help, afterlife. This sounds like something a self-help guru would say. Maybe if we comb through some of the titles, we can find a match?"

No one else offered anything.

They all stared at each other for the next ten minutes and threw out random ideas, but none of it felt right to Avery, and she imagined the pieces of the puzzle moving further and further apart.

CHAPTER ELEVEN

The intense day finally caught up to Avery on the drive home. All of a sudden, she found herself on her old street, driving to her old apartment in South Boston.

Whoa, she thought.

Quickly, she turned and headed in the right direction.

After her last case, Avery had not only upgraded her ride, but she'd also realized it would be better—both mentally and physically—if she moved into a completely new section of town. Although she'd always admired her last apartment, it was filled with too many memories of her former life; she'd bought it right after leaving her power job at Seymour & Finch, and the one and only time her daughter, Rose, had visited, the first sentence out of her mouth was: "This place is dark and miserable; it feels like somewhere people go to die."

Her new home was on Claremont Street in the Columbus district of Boston. The money from her last apartment had allowed her to buy an even bigger two-bedroom space that, in the daytime, boasted bright sunlight from three directions and an outdoor terrace. Combined with the many windows, it made Avery feel like a completely different person.

She parked in the lot and headed up.

The open expanse of her huge new home was filled with boxes, countless boxes that hadn't been opened. Boxes in the bedroom contained her clothing and a single mattress had been thrown on the floor with a sheet and blanket to sleep. Still, Avery couldn't get over how far she'd come. The new place and her new ride were such a far cry from the life she left behind in Ohio. Every time she felt lost or down, she would think of it. *You came from nothing,* she told herself, *and then you became a high-powered lawyer and now a cop. Remember that.*

Exhausted but still buzzed, Avery brushed her teeth and crashed on the mattress.

Sleep refused to take her.

The killer's note was fresh in her mind. She typed every word into her phone and searched for a match. Nothing came up.

Images bombarded her: the boat, the apartment, the fence across the street, all the books she'd seen on Venemeer's shelves, and the body with the hidden star and eerie shadow.

The kill might have been personal, she thought, *and the way the body was left harks to a serial killer. No one else leaves such a profound mark for no reason.*

She searched for new articles on her phone, not just from Boston but from across Massachusetts and surrounding states. She was looking for anything remotely related to what she'd observed on the yacht: a body placed in a certain way after death, possibly on water. Lots of images appeared from much older cases, all serial-killer related; none of them had the same feel from what she'd witnessed.

She put her phone to the side.

She stared at the ceiling.

What are you missing? she wondered.

An old, familiar voice returned to her mind: "You have to think like a killer, Avery. He won't want to be *caught*, but he'll be so excited to tell you everything. You have to think like him to see between the lines."

Although Howard Randall was a psychotic murderer that had nearly destroyed her life, Avery had felt a strange connection to him over the past five years. The term "mentor" rang true to their union. Her father had never been a real father; her mother was even worse. The foster homes of her youth had done little but make her want to rebel against society. There had been mentors here and there: a high-school coach that helped her get into college; Jane Seymour, the head lawyer at Seymour & Finch; and Howard.

You don't need Howard to solve this murder or any other, she inwardly fought. *True,* she realized. *But he always follows your cases. And what he gleans from papers alone is fascinating. Maybe he can offer some insight.*

She laughed at the idea.

At what price? she wondered. *You said goodbye. Let him go.*

Still, she couldn't shake the idea.

The papers will have a field day with you, So what? They do already. O'Malley will kill you. Randall might be able to help! Check out Venemeer's friends and workers first, she urged. *Exhaust every angle before you make a really stupid mistake.*

Her head lay on the pillow.

Eyes open, she stared at the wall and mulled her options.

CHAPTER TWELVE

He took meticulous notes scribbled on paper in shorthand, and he went over everything after his task was complete. *Camera on that street. Big-nosed woman always walks her dog at night. Building two has security checks and cameras.*

A detailed blueprint came to his mind, like the universe with bright stars and a dark background. The stars were people and security cameras and uncertain locations, and the darkness was the streets and buildings that were of no interest to him.

Suddenly, his body twitched, an involuntary reaction that he believed came from a series of drug treatments that had since proven ineffective. *Doctors*, he inwardly mumbled. *Liars. Every one of them. Only out for money. I've got a better prescription.*

At eleven twenty-two at night, he walked a few blocks north. A slight limp was evident in his gait. He headed into the Charles Street Station on the West End, which was encased in an ultra-modern glasswork structure. Despite the late hour, the station was full of people. The killer paid them no mind. None of the nameless bodies understood what he was doing, and none of them could control their fate. Not like him. He'd seen the signs.

He kept his head low to hide his face from the first camera as he swiped his card to enter. Instead of waiting for the train, he remained outside of camera view and stood by the glass wall, with his back turned toward the railroad.

He checked his watch.

Eleven thirty.

Through the blue-tinted glass of the station framework, he could clearly make out a low-rise apartment building in the distance.

At exactly eleven thirty-nine, he spotted something on the roof, a person and some kind of long object that jutted out from them.

He pulled military-grade binoculars out of his backpack and raised them.

Through the heightened vision, he could clearly see a tall, lean woman with straight blond hair on the roof. Her hands were around a black telescope. Every so often, she turned the lens and directed the scope to a particular spot in the sky, looked through, and then adjusted it. Once she finally found the object she was looking for, she was visibly placated, spending long moments staring through the lens.

He directed his binoculars to where the woman had pointed her telescope.

Stars were hard to see. He put down his binoculars and stared at the sky through the blue-tinted glass of the station. The stars had a calming effect on him.

With his naked eye, he observed the woman again.

I'm sorry, he thought. *It's the only way.*

And then, suddenly, everything turned red in his mind, a blood red that pumped his heart fast and made him look around from the sheer rush of adrenaline.

Don't you apologize to her, he mentally snapped. *She's the problem. Soon, she'll be the solution.*

CHAPTER THIRTEEN

A strange buzzing sound stirred Avery from her deep sleep.

Groggy and hungover, she peeked up. Sunlight filtered through her large bedroom window. She was flat on her stomach in nothing but a T-shirt.

The buzzing continued.

She checked her phone. It was well past nine—way later than she'd intended to sleep, and a lot later than she'd slept in a long, long time. She had five unanswered calls. Numerous text messages littered her phone. They were all from her daughter, Rose. *Are we still on for this morning? I'm on my way over. Hey, what's your street address again? I'm here! Where are you? Your car's out front so I know you're home! Mom! Answer my texts!*

Shit, Avery thought.

It was Thursday morning, the first day of her scheduled weekend, and Rose was supposed to come over and help her unpack.

Avery hopped up and threw on some shorts.

When she opened the front door, the joy that she felt over seeing her daughter on the other side was only dulled by the miserable expression on Rose's face.

"Where have you been?" Rose complained. "I've been calling and texting all morning."

Rose was the spitting image of Avery; they both had light-brown hair dyed blond, blue eyes, small noses, and high cheekbones. Only slightly shorter than Avery, she was dressed in overalls and a T-shirt in preparation for the day.

"I am *so sorry,*" Avery apologized.

She gave Rose a hug and pulled her in.

Rose sniffed the air.

"Are you drunk?" She frowned. "You smell like alcohol."

"No," Avery said. "I had a few drinks with the squad last night. I just woke up. I didn't even brush my teeth yet!"

"What happened to your face?"

"Ugh," Avery moaned. "Gang fight."

"*You* fought with a *gang*?"

Avery leaned back and put her hands on her hips.

"You know," she said, "my first three years on the force? When we rarely spoke? I fought with a *lot* of gangs, and I usually ended up on top."

"Who won this time?"

"Who do you think?" She smiled.

Rose nodded.

"Cool."

They stared at each other for a while. Rose eventually blushed and looked away and waved her hands around as if to erase the start of their meeting.

"OK, OK," she said. "I'm over it. Let's get started."

She walked past Avery and viewed the apartment for the first time.

"This place is huge!"

The expansive space was painted in a cream white. Floors were wooden. The living room was full of boxes, a couch, and a bookshelf. A large open kitchen was to the left and also cluttered with boxes. To the right was a hallway with two bedrooms and bathrooms.

The terrace door slid open and Rose stepped outside.

"This balcony is even bigger than your last one. How can you afford all this?"

Avery followed her out.

"I made some good investments when I was younger," she replied. "You and I should have that talk one day when you're ready to get a job. It's important."

"You still had money after Dad?"

Avery tilted her head and made a face.

"Yeah. I mean, I had to pay alimony and give him almost half of my paycheck, but he did take care of you during my meltdown years. It's all gone now, though. The new car and the apartment gobbled it up. Well, not your college fund." She smiled.

Rose leaned over the balcony and lowered her gaze. A foot kicked backward in a playful way and she rolled sideways to face Avery.

"Dad is single again," she said.

Inwardly, Avery groaned.

She'd been down this road before. When Rose was younger and the fights between Jack and Avery were already in full swing, that was all she'd ever heard: "Mom, why can't you make it work?" "Dad doesn't want to break up. Can't you try harder? Please? For me?" "Don't you *want* to keep the family together?"

The struggles had been endless.

It wasn't that Avery didn't love Jack; in many ways, she still did. When they'd met as freshmen at Boston University, he was a boundless spirit; fun and adventurous and always looking on the bright side of life. The arrival of Rose had changed everything.

Well, Avery had to admit, *you were the one that changed.* Jack's energy and enthusiasm simply weren't enough to handle a newborn child *and* allow Avery to continue her career goals. "I want to be a lawyer," she told him, "the best lawyer in Boston." "What about Rose?" he'd wondered. "And me? And *us?* Where do we fit into your grand plans?" The truth was, they hadn't. Marriage and a baby had arrived in a whirlwind and Avery simply hadn't been prepared for the sacrifice of her own dreams. In the end it was her dreams that had won out.

"Rose," she said, "I don't think your father would want me back."

"He talks about you all the time," she countered. "I mean, you were in every paper for like, a month! He followed your case every day. I swear, Mom, he has this lovesick look in his eyes whenever your name comes up. No one else compares to you."

A surprising feeling came to Avery at the thought of a relationship with Jack: hope. When they were together, he was so nice and accommodating and eager to please. Those traits had been inspiring when she was a student with her whole life ahead of her, but they'd turned into a grating mantra during law school.

Maybe he's changed, she thought. *I know I've changed.*

"Now's really not the right time," she said. "I'm in the middle of a big case. *Hey,*" she snapped to change the subject. "I thought you came over to help me unpack."

Rose spun around with a determined glint in her eyes.

"Not just yet," she said. "Make me a promise. You said you would come to my campus on Friday and check out Northeastern, right? What if I invited Dad along? He took me on the tour and he helped me move in, but now I know where all the cool spots are. We could have a picnic. Get some food, sit out on the lawn. What do you say?"

"Rose—"

"It's harmless, Mom. I mean, I'm only a five-minute drive from here. And when was the last time you two were in a room together? It's been years, right? Well, now you don't have to be in a room. You can be out in the open sunshine. Please," she begged and jumped into her arms. "Just this once? If things don't work out I'll never speak about it again."

Avery shook her head with a smile.

"You're very persuasive. You know that?"

"I take after my mom. Who knows? Maybe I'll even become a lawyer one day. I'm thinking about it. Northeastern has a great law school. So? Is that a yes?"

I guess it couldn't be that *bad,* Avery thought.

She hadn't seen Jack in ages. His positive attitude might even be a welcome change from the intense reality of Boston's underworld. For some reason, Ramirez popped into her mind. Avery sighed. *What are you going to do about* him*?*

"OK," she said. "Why not?"

"*Yes!*" Rose cheered.

Avery's phone was on the terrace table. A call came in. The ringer was on silent but the contact name was easy to see from where she stood: Seymour & Finch. The sight produced a feeling of nausea in Avery's core. Her face turned pale.

"What's wrong, Mom?"

Seymour & Finch, the mega–law firm that had hired her right out of law school to groom into the power attorney she'd become. Run by Jane Seymour and Danish Finch, the multimillion-dollar organization defended everyone from Boston's wealthiest patrons to the criminal elite.

"Is that your old law firm?" Rose said. "What could *they* want?"

"Let's find out," Avery said.

She picked up.

"Hello?"

"Hi, Avery? It's Jane! So glad you answered my call. How are you?"

For a long time, Jane Seymour was *the* woman that Avery had tried to mold herself into, a cutthroat, take-no-prisoners negotiator dressed in Armani suits with a smile that could make men swoon despite her advanced age.

"Hi, Jane. I'm good," Avery said with a terrified grimace at Rose. "What's up?"

"Listen, Avery. I'm going to get right to the point. We miss you. A lot has happened in the last few years, but everything has changed now. We want you back."

"You mean, you want me back at the firm?"

Rose widened her eyes and held her mouth.

"We think it was a mistake you left," Jane continued.

"You fired me, Jane."

"You were never *fired,*" Jane was quick to argue. "I don't know if you remember, but at the time, we *all* felt it would be mutually beneficial if we parted ways for a while. That was never meant to be forever, just until all the publicity died down. Well, now it has! You've won over the hearts and minds of the public again, Avery, and I for one, am so proud of you. Everyone in the office was following your last case. But let's be honest. Do you really want to be a police officer forever? Get your life back! Danish and I have already discussed it. You can come back at your same salary and take over like you never left. A spot just opened, and who knows what can happen in a few years. Maybe even partner. How does that sound? Seymour, Finch and Black? I like the ring of it, don't you?"

The offer was astounding, as well as surprising.

Never in a million years did Avery think she would get a personal call from Jane Seymour, a woman that had been like a mother to her, a mentor and confidant for all her years at the firm. That is, until Avery defended Howard Randall, the infamous Harvard professor accused of murder, and won. Only it turned out Randall was indeed the killer, and he killed again and then confessed to his crimes as some kind of sick way to tear Avery's life apart—and it had worked.

The days and weeks after Howard Randall surrendered to police had been a nightmare. Law firms across Boston and the country were in the crosshairs of every media outlet. "What kind of society do we live in," one newscaster had said, "when any criminal can be defended and released due to a good lawyer and a bad jury?" The negative publicity had come down the hardest on Seymour & Finch, a firm that had previously been in the news for similar defenses and acquittals of powerful Boston criminals. Howard Randall had been the last straw, and the only way the company could save its image was to offer up a sacrifice, someone that could take the blame for all their crimes.

"Wow," Avery said. "This is all so sudden. I don't know what to say."

"Don't say anything," Jane recommended. "Take some time. Think about it. This is a serious offer, Avery. A *firm* offer. What are you making now? Sixty-five? Seventy thousand tops? Is that the kind of life you want to live? You have a daughter to think about. Rose, right? And come on, you must miss our shopping adventures, right?"

Dollar signs tugged at Avery's soul.

She was making nothing now, pennies compared to what she'd made as an attorney. Still, the money wasn't her biggest issue. Rose's college was already paid, and in truth, Avery didn't need the money anymore. What mattered most to her now was justice. *Would I get that working at Seymour & Finch?* she thought. *No way. I'd be forced to defend the scum of the earth to earn my pay, and I can't do that any longer.* The image of Howard Randall came into her mind, as well as the sharp-dressed, quick-witted version of herself from her lawyer days. A glance at her new apartment and wardrobe made Avery realize that what she loved most now was making a difference, protecting the weak, and avenging the dead.

"Listen, Jane," she said, "I'll be honest. This offer is amazing, and I really appreciate it, but I don't need time to make my decision. The answer is no."

"Sleep on it," Jane laughed. "Talk to the family. See what happens. I'll call you back in a few days. I'm telling you, Avery, you're missing out on your true calling. You were the best I'd ever seen, except for myself, of course," she laughed. "And don't worry about Danish. He's fully on board. One hundred percent. We all want you back."

Avery glanced at Rose, who held up her arms as if to ask: *What's going on?*

You lost your life at that firm, Avery thought. *You forgot about Rose, you ignored Jack, you ruined your marriage, and eventually, it destroyed you. Now, you have your life back. Don't go down that road again. Make a clean break.*

"I do miss our shopping ventures together, Jane. And I miss your fighting spirit and aggressive attitude that would shock just about anyone. You're truly one of a kind. But that's about all I miss from the firm. The answer is still no, but if you ever want to grab lunch or help me elevate my detective wardrobe, I'm in."

"I'm really sorry to hear you say that, Avery. All right! Lord knows that when Avery Black makes a decision it's final. The offer still stands though. Keep it in mind, Avery. If you ever want your old job back, it's here."

"Thanks, Jane."

"No, thank *you*, Avery, for all your hard years of sacrifice."

Avery hung up the phone.

"Did you just turn down an offer from the biggest firm in Boston?" Rose asked.

"I think I did."

"You love being a cop that much?"

Detective, Avery thought. I'm a *detective* now. It wasn't a word that Avery had ever associated with herself as a child, or even as an adult. When she was young, getting out of Ohio and away from her parents had been her only goal. Law provided that and more. After Howard Randall, however, she was forced to rethink her views of the world, and herself. What she'd found was that it wasn't money or fame she was truly after, but justice. Being a detective allowed her to seek out justice, and to right all the wrongs that existed in the world. And, she got to carry a gun. *What more could a girl ask for?* she wondered.

"Yeah," she said. "I think I do love being a cop."

Rose offered a solemn nod.

"Well then," she said, "I guess I'm proud of you, Mom. That took a lot of guts. I don't know if I could have turned down an offer like that."

"Wait a while," Avery said. "The more you live, the more you learn, and trust me, you never know who you might become."

CHAPTER FOURTEEN

Throughout the morning and early afternoon, text messages kept popping up on Avery's phone from O'Malley and Connelly. "Did you figure out the riddle yet?" "Where are you on Venemeer's friends?" To top it off, the morning paper had another article on the harbor murder and the anonymous note from the killer. Avery had tried to clear her mind of everything. *I'm here with my daughter,* she thought, *who I never see. On my day off.* Still, it was nearly impossible not to think about the case.

By one o'clock, Rose was tanning on the balcony.

"Hey!" she called out. "Wanna grab some lunch?"

Avery's mind blared out: *Lunch!? You can't have lunch. You've got a killer on the loose. How much longer is this going to go on? Bonding time is over.*

"I don't think so," Avery said, "I need to get some work done."

"Work? I thought you had Thursday and Friday off."

"Technically, this is the start of my weekend," Avery said. "Realistically? I'm a cop, and cops chase killers, and killers keep no schedule for murder."

"Deep, Mom."

A call came in from Ramirez.

Eager to get back to work, Avery picked up.

"What's up?" she said.

"Yo, yo," he replied. "I know it's your day off and everything, so I don't want to bother you, but I spoke with two of Venemeer's best friends."

"Wait a minute," Avery said. "It's your day off too."

"True, true," he agreed. "But you inspire me, Black. You're a star detective that just took out six guys in a gang den and couldn't even relax at a bar afterwards to celebrate. If I'm going to be your partner, and maybe more," he softly added in a shy, reserved tone, "I've got to show you I'm all in, all the time—just like you."

The sentiment touched her. Avery didn't think anyone was as dedicated as her when it came to tracking criminals. The fact that Ramirez wanted to up his game, even after the conversation they'd had the night before, gave her a warm, fuzzy feeling. *Maybe I put the brakes on our relationship too fast,* she thought. *Maybe this can work.*

"I'm impressed," she said. "What did you find?"

"Couldn't sleep last night," he replied. "I was up at six. So I called Simms and touched base. Went back to Venemeer's

58

apartment, looked through her personal effects, photographs, checked through a list of phone calls Simms had compiled, and came up with two best friends that she routinely either saw or phoned. One of them is the manager of the bookshop. She said most of the employees are all new, only in the last year or so, and she swore none of them could commit a crime. She suggested we go further back, to people that worked there three to five years ago. She said there were a bunch of wackos that Venemeer had to deal with when she first opened. I'm going to check them out next."

Avery watched Rose out on the balcony.

"Great work," she said.

"There's more," he went on. "The second friend confirmed everything the first one had said, and she also mentioned that Venemeer changed hobbies and interests every year or so. Last year she was into cats and puppies, so she ordered a lot of those books at the shop. The year before that it was dating advice because she'd just come out of a bad relationship. She gave me the name of that boyfriend. He's on the list too."

"You got far," Avery said. "You hit the one checklist *I* was supposed to hit."

"You wanna ride with me?" he asked. "I know you're not just chilling out after that note from the killer. You figure it out yet?"

No, Avery thought. *I haven't figured it out.*

The face of Howard Randall invaded her thoughts, the old and wrinkled man with his Coke-bottle glasses, thinning hair, and powerful, observant eyes.

"Haven't made any headway on the letter," she said. "Not sure about the rest of the day. I thought I might consult with a professional."

"A professional? Who?"

"You don't want to know."

"I *do* want to know. Who?"

"Howard Randall," she said.

"Are you crazy!? That guy ruined your life. He set you up! I never understood why you conferred with him on the Peet case."

"I can't explain it," she said.

"Are the papers true?" he asked. "Did you...you know?"

"No!" Avery shouted. "Nothing like that. He's just like a... This is going to sound stupid so you'd better not laugh."

"I won't laugh."

"He's like a father figure to me."

Saying the words aloud somehow offered Avery a well of relief.

"I never really had a father," she went on. "I know it's crazy. Believe me. I know. But part of him, in some strange way, *cares* about me."

"I'm not going to lie and say I understand it."

"I'm not asking you too."

"Still," Ramirez said, "I trust you. You've taken a lot of heat over that relationship, so it must be important. You really think he can help?"

Avery bit her nail.

"We'll see."

CHAPTER FIFTEEN

Howard Randall appeared to have aged since the last time Avery had seen him. There was a slump in his shoulders, and the grayish coloring and lines of his face made him seem much older than his fifty-some-odd-years. They sat in a bland, gray conference room on B-Level, reserved for the most dangerous prisoners that were confined to solitary. He wore an orange jumpsuit and his hands were cuffed to the table before him.

"I *knew* you'd come back," he whispered with his head low. "I'm so glad to see you, Avery. What happened to your face?"

"Gang fight," she said.

"Gang fight?" he asked, worried. "With whom?"

"Juan Desoto. A killer-for-hire with his own crew."

"He did that to your face?" Howard asked.

"Yup."

"Hmmm."

"Why are you still on B-Block?" Avery said.

Howard met her gaze with childish glee.

"Prison is a funny place," he replied, "a *fascinating* place. Out beyond those walls—in a world I truly used to love—I was so confined, so set in my ways. I see that now. Here, anything is possible. We live in one big petri dish, one large experiment, only there are no repercussions for your actions. You can kill someone in here, stab them, bash their brains out, and where do you go? Nowhere. Here. To B-Block. Still in prison. Still getting the same food. Still sleeping in a nice bed. Out in the real world, there was always a fear of being caught, of being *known*. Here, everyone knows who I am."

"You didn't answer my question."

He lifted his chin and tried to wave it away.

"Nothing serious," he said. "I used my own hands to puncture the esophagus of an extremely foul-mouthed young man. Skin is extremely tough. Did you know that? I pulled out his throat and offered it to a Santa Muerte worshipper. He was very grateful, of course. The guards, however, they were alarmed by my blood-smeared body. I think they're afraid of me," he whispered. "Can you imagine that? Afraid of an old man?"

"You're sick," she whispered.

"You *missed* me."

"Not even a little," she lied. "I came back because I need your help."

"The harbor case." He nodded. "Yes, I know."

"How do you know?"

"Jail is a lot like the real world, Avery. Anything you want can be had, *at a price*," he emphasized and watched her for a reaction.

"Well," she said. "What do you think about the case?"

Randall eased back into his seat. His eyes squinted in observation of Avery, and then he casually glanced around the room.

"After your mother was killed and your father went away to prison, where did *you* go?" he wondered. "What did you do? That part of your life is absent in public records."

Talking to Randall always kept Avery on edge. A part of her knew she could never trust him. *What does he already know about me?* she wondered. *Is he trying to catch me in a lie, or does he really want to know about my life?*

"I was put in an orphanage," she said. "Well," she clarified, "they didn't call it an orphanage at the time. Foster care was the term. I became a ward of the state."

Concern crossed Randall's face.

"You had no guardians, no other family?"

"Not really. I never met my grandparents. My father had two brothers but they all hated each other and they lived in separate states, so we never saw them. My mother had a sister that never liked me or my father or anyone, so we were on our own."

"How sad," Randall said.

The deep, emotional reaction he seemed to have affected Avery in a way she hadn't expected. She had spent years dealing with her childhood in therapy, but Randall's tear-filled gaze brought it all back: the foster home fights, the abuse, the constant degradation by the other children and the staff. "No one will ever want you," one woman had said. "Your father was a murderer and your mother was crazy. You'll probably be crazy too." "You're too old," said another care worker. "Nobody wants kids over ten. They all want the babies. Prepare to stay here for a long, long time."

"How did you survive?" Randall asked. "What did you do?"

Avery opened her mouth to casually offer her foster-home success story. The words caught in her throat.

No, she told herself. *Don't go there.*

Memories rushed back, painful memories. A group of kids had hounded her during those first few months. "*Father-killer, mother-dead; father-killer, mother-dead!*" they would chant. One of them, a boy named Blake who was two years younger and shorter than Avery, picked on her constantly. "If your daddy was a murderer, you're probably a murderer, so I should kill you now!" He punched her in the face and threw her to the ground.

Suddenly, Avery was in tears.

There had been so much she'd dealt with in therapy, so many memories brought to the surface and rehashed and expelled and yet still, here she was, a mess. *When will it end?* she wondered. *When does the pain go away?*

Howard waited patiently, silently, until the episode was over. The empathy on his face made it easier for Avery to wipe her tears and recover. She braced herself for more questions. Instead, Randall glanced away.

"He gave you the cycle," he said. "I'm surprised you didn't see it right away. *First body* doesn't necessarily refer to the victim. What else is a body?"

He stared at her, and she wracked her brain so long, it hurt. Was Howard playing her? Or was he really hinting at something? Somehow she sensed he knew the answer—and that made it all the more frustrating.

"Think, Avery, think."

CHAPTER SIXTEEN

A wreck.

That's how Avery felt when she left Randall: like a complete and utter wreck. She thought those days, that time in her life, had been forgotten. *No*, she realized. *You didn't try to forget. You tried to erase it completely from your life.* They were back now. That single memory brought others to the surface. *Get out,* she thought. *Get out of my head!*

The only way she could make it stop was to focus on Howard and his riddle. He never used words lightly. He was a former Harvard professor, and everything had a double meaning or some hidden meaning or more than one meaning.

He said "He gave you the cycle," she thought. *What cycle? What has a cycle? What else is a body?* she wondered and mentally referred back to the victim.

There was a star over her body.

Cycles...

Bodies...

Planets, she thought. *Could it be planets? They go through cycles. They're referred to as bodies. There was a star drawn over her body.*

The more she thought it through, the more it seemed like a solid, viable option. The letter came back to her: "The first body is set." *If he's referring to a planet,* she realized, *he could be an astronomer, or a stargazer, or something like that. Where do astronomers hang out?*

Ramirez was in the parking lot, leaning on his own car and deep in thought. At the sight of Avery, he offered an enthusiastic wave.

"Hey!" he called.

"What are *you* doing here?" She smiled.

"Came to see you," he said. "I got something."

Ramirez was in full weekend gear: tan slacks, light-blue linen, button-down T-shirt, and loafers without socks. A twinkle sparked in his dark eyes and he had a semi-grin on his face, and for a second, Avery wanted to give him a big hug.

"What did you learn?" she asked.

Ramirez noticed her initial excitement at seeing him, then her hesitation and shutdown. He, in turn, wiped off his smile and played it cool.

"I talked to the former boyfriend of Venemeer, plus two people that used to work there. Nothing there. Still two more people left to check out but I'm not sure. Everybody keeps saying the same thing: Venemeer could be a real bitch. Always had to be in control. Would give money to homeless people and work at shelters, but if she wasn't in charge, there would be friction. The boyfriend and former employees I spoke with? And I mean all of them? Said that at least once a month they'd get into an argument over something. Maybe they would say something wrong, or try to help her out of a bad situation, and Venemeer would freak out, whatever. None of them had records, and they all had some strong alibis for the night of the murder."

Avery was barely focused on what he was saying.

"Excellent," she mumbled, her mind on astrology.

"You learn anything from *him*?" Ramirez said and pointed to the prison.

"I'm not sure yet. Want to take a ride? I'll drop you off later."

"Where to?"

"The Observatory."

CHAPTER SEVENTEEN

The Judson B. Coit Observatory on Commonwealth Avenue was well known to Avery. It was the only true stargazing dome in Boston, and it was part of Boston University, where she'd attended college. Once or twice, her ex-husband, Jack, had tried to lure her into the Arts & Sciences Building so they could drink wine and view the stars, alone on the roof. Avery had never been interested. Heights frightened her, and staring at the sky for too long had always filled her with too many questions about the universe that she couldn't answer. She preferred to keep her feet on the ground and her mind on the present.

Back on her old stomping grounds near Fenway Park, Avery turned off Commonwealth and parked at the back of the A&S Building. She'd taken one required course there during her tenure, so she was familiar with how to reach the Observatory.

They walked up five flights to the top floor. The stairs opened into a large, brick-lined area with benches and pictures of the universe. Students ambled about, and a tour guide was in the middle of a presentation.

"Now we move on to..."

The main observatory room was similar to the waiting area in the hall: extremely large, brick-lined, with numerous desks. There was a large, floor-to-ceiling whiteboard with a ladder-on-wheels so the professor could position it wherever they wanted. A few students sat alone doing research before a wall of computers.

A second level was visible from the floor. Avery looked up to see a circular opening in the ceiling, protected by a wooden banister. Above it was a domed area, and beyond that lay the roof and observatory.

She jogged up a spiral staircase and was quickly followed by Ramirez. More students were on the next level, taking notes while being led by a tour guide. Avery scanned the walls. Numerous sayings in Latin were inscribed in stone. Pictures lined the area. One in particular seemed to be of all the astronomy professors, past and present.

"The Observatory was originally located on Boylston Street," the guide was saying. "It was named after the first professor of astronomy appointed at Boston University. It's not just used by undergraduate and graduate programs. People from all over the state come here to study the stars."

Avery continued up.

A door opened to the roof.

Something like a beat-up trailer was located on top, right beside a white-domed viewing station. Inside the small shack was a workshop. Two long, wooden tables on either side were stuffed with tool boxes, soldering equipment, duct tape, adhesives, metal, wood, and countless other items. On the walls and shelves were tuning forks and various light bulbs and telescope parts and tools.

A middle-aged man with black, graying hair was perched on a stool. He wore overalls and a black T-shirt and was deeply engaged with what appeared to be a grimy generator. He tried to unscrew a part, but the bolt had been stripped.

"Excuse me," Avery said.

The man startled and turned. He was handsome, slightly tanned, and agitated.

"I'm sorry," he said, "you can't be up here."

He prepared to go back to work.

"We're police," Ramirez said.

Avery offered her badge. Ramirez showed his.

"Oh," the man said. A quick lean forward and he squinted and spoke both of their badge numbers out loud.

"I have a photographic memory," he said of their curious expressions. "This way, if I ever need to reach one of the two police officers that accosted me on my roof, I can find you."

"We're sorry to bother you like this," Avery said. "I'm Detective Black, and this is my partner, Detective Ramirez."

"Peter Landing," he said, "I'm one of the astronomy professors here at Boston University. Today," he sighed, "I'm acting as the observatory assistant. Can't get this generator to work," he mumbled and turned back to his desk to work again, until he remembered Avery and Ramirez were standing there, and he slowly swiveled his chair around.

"How long have you worked here?"

"Going on twenty years," he said, as if just realizing that fact.

"What do you do here?" Avery asked.

"Besides *teach* astronomy?" He laughed. "That's a very good question. The lectures are only a small fraction of my day, that's true. I also prepare the labs for the students. Well," he countered, "my assistant typically prepares the labs. You know, concrete, hands-on science? So students can actually witness firsthand what's happening up in the universe? Things like that. Take light, for example," he said. "This semester we had a lab where students studied the light reflected off rocks. The idea was to show them that planets and moons with similar rocks would emit a similar light across the universe, you see?"

"What's the purpose of that?" Ramirez wondered.

"Well, light is the only way we *see* other planets and observe other stars."

"Ah," Ramirez noted, "I see."

"Do you?" Landing honestly wondered.

Avery pointed to the sky.

"Can you see anything in the daytime?"

Landing came to life.

"Yes, of course," he said. "Obviously, light from our sun dilutes the sky so during the day it appears as if there are no stars directly above. But there are. We can see some of them in the day, but we can also see a host of other objects: the sun, the moon, planets, even satellites. Would you like to take a look?"

"Sure," Avery said. "Are we going in there?"

She pointed to the large white dome.

"No need for that," he said. "The dome is only used to help drown out the light during night viewings. Since we're looking at the sky in the daytime, we can use one of these."

He pointed to three telescopes that had already been set up.

"A class earlier today was observing the moon. Might have to make a slight adjustment," he said as he fiddled with one of the telescopes and peered through. "There we go," he said. "You can see a waning crescent right now, about three-quarters full. Take a look."

With a wave, he stepped back.

Avery had never seen anything through a telescope before. A friend growing up had owned one, but he'd never figured out how to view anything, so all she'd observed was darkness. A giddy feeling came over her, like a child about to enter a fun new ride.

She closed one eye and pressed the other one against the rubber eyepiece.

The gray orb that appeared in her view was spectacular to behold, a large object lit by the sun and surrounded by blue sky. Darker circles of flat land could be seen, along with splatter holes and white-tipped mountains and rocks.

"Wow," she said. "Incredible."

Ramirez took a look next.

"I assume you didn't come all the way here to look at the moon," Landing said.

"Yes, that's true." Avery smiled. "We're hoping you can help us find someone. We're in the middle of an investigation and we

68

have reason to believe a suspect might have worked at this observatory, or came to BU to study astrology. Is there anyone you can remember in all your years that really stood out as a potential problem? Maybe someone that was kicked out for aggression, or a student that seemed dangerous in some way?"

Landing scratched his head.

"You do realize that over ten *thousand* people *work* at this school each year, and we have nearly thirty-five *thousand* undergraduates and graduates, *each year*," he stressed.

"Well"—Avery smiled—"since you have a photographic memory, that shouldn't be much of a problem for you, should it?"

Landing laughed.

"Very funny," he said. "So you want me to help you find a student or professor that was either kicked out or somehow stood out as aggressive among the thousands of people that I happen to know, is that right?"

A dawning realization came to Avery. The Observatory had been a long shot to begin with, but with the knowledge of the actual number of visitors and students, she wondered: *What if he didn't stand out at all? What if he came here but was invisible?*

She tried to rally.

"That's right," she said.

Landing clapped and stood up from his seat. He was short and wiry, and he slid in between the two of them like they weren't there. On the black roof, he put his hands behind his back and began to pace.

"Sorry," he said, "I think more clearly when I'm walking. Now let's see. If you're trying to find someone, we should narrow down the parameters. You say it's a man. Do you have an approximate age?"

"Could be anywhere from thirty to sixty," Ramirez said.

Avery nodded in agreement.

"Hm," Landing mumbled, "any personality traits you can offer?"

"Angry," Avery said. "He's angry, and he feels somehow connected to the stars. Maybe someone pushed him on a point and he disagreed. He might have lashed out."

"Not very many aggressive students in the astronomy program." Landing smiled. "Connected to the stars," he echoed. "Now that's interesting. Do you know anything about the stars and planets?"

They both shook their heads.

"Then you're at a distinct disadvantage from your suspect, I believe. A quick lesson, you see, is that astronomy is all about the universe, the planets, stars, clusters—whatever we can find up there using math and a telescope. Everything has a pattern, a very distinct signature. For example, all of the planets in our solar system revolve around the sun. Stars move, but they move very slowly in conjunction with the universe around them. Astronomers study the light and patterns and try to make observations about things that we *can't* see, from what we *can*."

Patterns, Avery thought. *What if he's killing in a pattern?*

The placement of the body became even more important, as well as the angle of her body, and the shadow and the star.

Could he have been indicating a certain constellation?

Ramirez rubbed his head.

"What does this have to do with angry students?" he wondered.

"Nothing." Landing brightened. "But if you're searching for an angry former student that might have done something wrong, and you came to the Observatory, then you think whatever he's done is somehow connected to the cosmos, and if that's the case, you might want to learn a thing or two about the subject."

Slighted, Ramirez opened his mouth to fire back.

"That's a very good point," Avery said with a stern look at her partner. "However, is there anything you can remember about a particular student or professor?"

Landing straightened his back and put a finger to his chin.

"I'm going to be honest," he said. "There's only one boy that really stands out in my mind that matches your description. Whether he's a killer or not I can't say. He was here about two years ago. Dark hair, blue eyes. Very unnerving young man. My assistant at the time was a young girl named Molly and she swore this boy was up to no good. She had no real reason for the claim, but then the director of the Observatory threw him out when he attacked another student during a night viewing session. After that, I heard he was thrown out of the school."

"Do you have a name?" Avery asked.

Landing's eyes moved from side to side.

"John," he recalled. "John Deluca. But," he added quickly with a frown at both of them, "you shouldn't really form a suspect based on the memories of one man and a situation that occurred years earlier. If I were you, I would check with the registrar, and maybe even meet with the dean to see about other aggressive instances on campus. Otherwise, this connection seems a bit weak to me, don't you think?"

Ramirez checked his phone.

"Not that weak," he said, and showed Avery the name *John Deluca* on his notepad. "That's one of the names Venemeer's friend gave me. One I hadn't checked out yet. A real creeper that used to work in her shop. His name is John Deluca."

CHAPTER EIGHTEEN

"It *can't* be a coincidence," Avery said when they were back in the car.

"I just can't believe your boy Randall came through for you." Ramirez howled. "Who would have thought that Howard Randall would give you some honest intel?"

Avery pointed at her dashboard computer.

"See what you can find on Deluca. If he's not in the system, we'll split up. You'll take the registrar at BU and I'll head to Venemeer's bookstore. If he worked there, they paid him checks so his address should be on file."

Her car computer came with the same identification system they had in the office, only with a higher security system because it often used an unsecure wireless account.

Ramirez typed on the keyboard.

"Got him," he said.

The police mug shot showed an angry, agitated young man, most likely on illegal or prescription drugs. He had unclean, wavy black hair and blue eyes, a narrow neck, and emaciated cheeks.

"Looks just like Landing said he would," Avery realized.

"Now does that look like the face of a killer or does that look like the face of a killer?" Ramirez excitedly asked.

"Known address," Avery mumbled and read.

She backed out of the lot and took off.

Ramirez scrolled through the docket.

"Hmmm," he said. "This sheet is seven years old. Says here he was caught in a brawl on the BU campus. That must be why he was kicked out. He was on probation for two years. This address was updated from his school dorm. Let's hope he's still there."

"Anything else?"

"Nothing since then. But that doesn't mean he's innocent. I mean, he was fired from Venemeer's shop. That's big, right? Maybe we should call for backup."

"Why?"

Ramirez twisted his face.

"What's with you and no backup?"

In her mind, Avery returned to one of her foster centers, being beaten and kicked by her childhood tormentor. Everyone in the room was yelling: "*Get her! Kick her. She thinks she's better than everyone else. Not so great now, are you, Black?*" The entire time, a girl Avery had thought was her best friend stood by and did nothing.

No backup then, she thought. *No backup at Desoto's. No backup now.*

"This is a routine Q&A," she answered. "His name came up on the suspect list, we went to his house to investigate. No reason to call in the troops just yet."

The address led Avery to a suburban street in East Roslindale. Houses were nicely spaced apart, with front lawns and garages. The house in question was a dilapidated, three-story corner home. Work was being done on the property. Elevated about four feet from the street, it had a stone wall around the entire area. The lawn had been replaced by gravel.

"Nice house," Ramirez joked.

Avery had a strange feeling. All the boxes checked: John Deluca worked at Venemeer's shop. He was an astronomy major that was kicked out. The victim's body had a star drawn above it. The house, however, didn't fit. *This looks like a family house,* Avery thought. *Maybe it's his parents', or it was left to him in a will.*

They parked on the street and walked up the steps to the front door.

A very sweet, middle-aged woman answered the door. She was small, with cropped blond hair and rosacea on her cheeks.

"Hi there!" she cheerily said. "What can I do for you?"

Both of them flashed their badges.

"Is this the house of John Deluca?" Avery asked.

"Why, yes, it is," she said with a frown. "Is something wrong?"

"Is he home?" Avery asked.

"Yes, he is."

"Can we talk to him?"

The woman became smaller and more guarded.

"I'm not sure," she muttered and glanced inside the house.

"Miss, please," Ramirez said. "Your son is not in trouble. We are on a routine case and would just like to ask him a few questions."

Her shoulders slumped and she glanced up at them with a downturned chin.

"Did he do something?" she asked in a whisper.

Avery and Ramirez shared a look.

"Miss, please," Ramirez said.

She opened the door.

"He's downstairs," she mumbled. "He lives downstairs. Would you mind if I came down? He doesn't always react well to visitors."

"Are you his mother?" Avery asked. "Ms. Deluca?"

"Yes." She brightened. "I am. But you can call me Suzie."

"Thank you, Suzie. I'm curious. Do you usually know when your son comes and goes from the house?"

"Of course," she said, flustered. "We're on a schedule. He *has* to be on a schedule, otherwise he gets very confused and emotional."

They moved over a brown rug and into a yellow-painted kitchen. A wooden door led to the basement. Suzie slowly took the lead and held onto the wooden banister.

The basement was a dark and bizarre space, lit only by a couple of bulbs that hung from the ceiling, the entire floor matted with a black carpet. Planets hung from the ceiling, so many that it took Avery a minute to realize it was supposed to be the Milky Way galaxy, and then other galaxies and stars. Puffy white cotton balls had been grouped together and dotted with blue to form gaseous clusters. The walls were all painted black and dotted with stars and painted with other galaxies and planets. There was a bed and table and bookshelf but they were all insignificant compared to the wild depiction of the universe that filled the dark void.

"Jesus," Ramirez whispered.

He kept his hand on his gun.

A young man sat on the floor with a flashlight, deeply immersed in a book. Even from his seated position, he appeared tall and gaunt. The unclean black hair matched the picture from his mug shot. He wore black sweatpants that made him seem like half a body against the black carpet, and an old white T-shirt. Avery tried to look for shoes to see about a fit.

"Johnny," his mother called. "You have some guests here."

Only the flashlight pen moved.

A book page was turned.

"Johnny? They're police officers. Did you do anything wrong lately?"

His body crunched up suddenly. The book and pen dropped and his hands seemed to curl into each other.

"*I'm not!*" he slurred. "*I'm not. I'm not!*"

"Johnny, it's OK," his mother cooed and went to his side. "It's OK, honey. They just want to talk, that's all."

Deluca swayed in his spot. His mother hugged his shoulders.

"It's OK, she said, "it's OK."

"What do they want?!" he cried in the same slurring voice.

He's special, Avery realized.

"Just a few questions," his mother said, and she waved them on. "You can come closer. He's all right. He's just used to being alone."

Avery squatted down beside him. Shoes: Ten and a half or eleven, she thought. A match. Deluca swayed back and forth. His hands curled and his mouth was in a sneer.

"Hi there, John," Avery whispered. "How are you today?"

"*No!*" he yelled.

"It's OK, Johnny."

"John," Avery went on, "I'd like to ask you about a bookstore where you used to work. Do you remember? It was run by a woman named Henrietta Venemeer?"

"Ha, ha ha," Deluca laughed.

"Oh yes." Suzie smiled. "He worked there for about three months. They had a disagreement over something related to astronomy and I'm afraid Johnny got very upset. He threw down one of the bookshelves and became extremely angry. They didn't feel safe there, so they had to let him go. But you would never hurt anyone, would you, baby?"

Deluca smiled and hugged her.

"Thanks, Mom."

"What happened at Boston University?" Avery asked.

"That was the same kind of thing." Suzie frowned. "I was actually very upset with the dean because they knew about his condition right from the start. Johnny had excellent grades in high school and even as an undergraduate. As long as he was on his medicine and being handled properly, he was just fine. I blame the college. He had one incident. That's all. Just one," she firmly stated. "And all of a sudden he was expelled. I thought of suing."

"Can I ask what he did?"

"He liked a *girl*," she said as if it were no big deal. "And he never expresses himself properly. He keeps his feelings inside and he waits and waits and then they just burst right out. Well, they burst out in an astronomy class. He told her he loved her. Tried to kiss her. Unfortunately, she had a boyfriend and Johnny attacked him. Again, it wasn't really his fault. That girl must have led him on somehow, must have made him think *something.* And that boy had a bunch of friends join in the fight. Terrible, just terrible. None of *them* were expelled."

"Do you know where your son was on Tuesday night?" Avery asked.

"Of course," Suzie said. "The same place he is every night. Right here with me."

"Can you verify that?"

"Well," she said. "Let's see. Tuesday. My sister was over on Tuesday. You can contact her if you like. I'm sure she'll tell you the same thing I did."

"One more question," Ramirez said. "What shoe size does your son wear?"

Suzie indicated a pair of sneakers by the wall.

"Twelve," she said. "Why?"

Avery's heart fell. This was not their guy.

CHAPTER NINETEEN

"That was crazy," Ramirez said in the car.

"No one gave you any indication he was special needs?" Avery asked.

"Well, one of them said he was *special*, but she was like 'he was a real special kind of asshole.' You know? What am I supposed to do with that?"

"Dammit," Avery muttered.

It was getting late, and a lead she thought would solve the case had turned out to be nothing. Once again, as always, she began to question Randall's integrity. *Why would he lie? He* doesn't *lie,* she told herself. *He just never gives you a straight answer.*

So close, she berated herself. *So close.*

Her phone rang. The name on the screen made her heart stop and the color drain from her face: Jack. Her ex-husband. They hadn't spoken in over a year.

What could he *want?*

Avery hopped out of the car.

"Give me a second," she said to Ramirez.

"What is it?"

Avery held up her palm and kept walking with the phone by her ear.

"Hey," she said in her happiest voice. "How are you?"

The voice on the other end was less enthusiastic.

"Hi, Avery," he replied in a banal tone, "thanks for taking my call. Listen, do you mind meeting me for coffee or something tonight? I know it's late and you're probably on call, but I feel like we should sit down and hash some things out."

"What's wrong? Is it Rose? What happened?"

"Rose is fine. Nothing terrible has happened. I just want to talk, and you know I hate talking on the phone. Every time we're on the phone, we have a fight."

"That's not true."

He ignored her.

"I'm thinking our old spot," he said, "hang out for a while, get some coffee, talk? It would be like old times. I'd be lying if I said I didn't miss you."

"Yeah," she said, "of course," and she instinctively brushed back a lock of hair. "Are you around now? I can be there in fifteen or twenty minutes. No," she corrected and glanced at Ramirez still sitting in her car. *Have to drop him off,* she remembered. "Scratch that. I have to make one more stop. How about forty-five minutes?"

"That would be perfect," he said. "It's good hearing your voice, Avery. Looking forward to seeing you."

Avery hung up with a light, happy feeling in her core.

Jack, she thought.

His voice had sounded different, sad and guarded. *What do you expect?* she argued. *You haven't spoken in ages. You broke his heart countless times. He doesn't trust you.* The picnic that Rose wanted to do the following day now seemed entirely plausible. *You're going to see him tonight. What if things go well? Second date tomorrow?* She smiled and was shocked at her own girlish excitement. She felt like a college freshman again, about to meet the man of her dreams. *This is ridiculous,* she thought. *It's just coffee. One step at a time.*

"Who was that?" Ramirez asked.

"Nobody."

He was about to say something and thought better of it.

Avery drove him back to the prison parking lot. They were nearly silent the entire way.

"You wanna grab some dinner tonight?" he asked.

Avery lowered her head.

"I can't," she said. "Not tonight. Maybe tomorrow?"

"Yeah," he replied, disappointed. "Maybe."

He scrunched his lips and opened his door.

"Dan," she called.

Hopeful, he looked back.

"Yeah?"

Handsome, she thought, *so sweet and handsome and he cares about me.*

"Nothing," she said. "Sorry. Thanks for today. We'll get him. We'll follow up on those other names and figure it out. I know we will."

His face fell.

"Sure," he said.

CHAPTER TWENTY

The diner was a small, unusual place on the corner of Columbus Avenue. The white exterior was paneled in glass and surrounded by larger brownstones.

Avery sat in a booth and stared out the window.

Drunken college students sat in a booth behind her. One of them had ordered a hamburger with beans, bacon, eggs, and he devoured it while two of his friends appeared ready to puke from the massive inhalation of food.

A dark, cloudy night sky was visible through the window. A quick flash of light appeared, then the rumble of thunder.

"Hey," someone said.

Jack stood overhead with a guarded smile on his face. *Just as handsome as always,* Avery thought. He had shaggy brown hair cut short in the back. He had piercing eyes and stubble on his face. A brown leather jacket was open over a teal-colored shirt. A strong chest and lean stomach were obvious.

"Hey." Avery smiled. "Take a seat."

Jack sat in the booth and took a moment to gaze at her features.

"You look good," he said. "Except for the—" And he indicated the bruises that still marred her features.

"Yeah," she flirted, "gang fight. You know how it is."

Ugh, she thought. *Settle down. This isn't a date.*

"I can't even imagine," he seriously replied. "It's incredible what you do now. I never would have believed it."

"Small-town girl living a big-time life." She smiled.

"I appreciate you coming here," Jack said.

"I was surprised you wanted to meet," she admitted. "Glad, but surprised, especially since we're supposed to have a picnic tomorrow, right?"

"Yeah," he mumbled and lowered his gaze, "that's what I wanted to talk about."

A waiter appeared.

"You want to order something?" Avery asked.

"No," he said. "Well, maybe a milk?"

"Milk?" Avery laughed. "Since when do you drink milk?"

"Milk," he said to the waiter and then indicated Avery. "For you?"

"I'll have coffee. Just coffee."

"You won't be able to sleep," Jack mentioned.

The words made Avery bristle. One of the biggest fights they'd consistently had was his inability to let her live her life. The desire to "fix" her had been never-ending. No matter what was happening—it could be over something as mundane as coffee or a larger issue like deciding on a career path—Jack would offer his opinion, whether it was asked for or not, and then uphold a superior attitude if she chose something different.

"Coffee," she reiterated to the waiter.

Jack raised his brows and shrugged.

"Been following you in the papers," he said.

"Don't believe everything you read."

"I believe you're a hero," he said with an honest, intense gaze. Seriously, I'm impressed. When you left the law firm and said you wanted to be a cop? I thought you were crazy. But now?" He nodded. "You really did it, and it suits you. You look happy. You do."

"Thanks, Jack," she said with a hint of suspicion. "I *am* happy. Overworked, beat up, and tired, but happy. It's been a long time since I could say that."

"Yeah," he said. "I know."

Silence filled the air. The group behind them burst out laughing and Avery tried to think of something, anything, to say."

"How about you?" she asked.

"I'm good," he replied. "I'm in advertising now."

"I heard. Congratulations, Rose told me. I never had you pegged as an advertiser."

"I'm good at it," he said. "Coming up with pitches, different angles for commercials and print ads. It's fun. Pays the bills and takes my mind off other things."

"No more outdoors for you?"

A sly smile gave him a debonair appearance.

"Are you kidding?" he said. "I'm out every weekend. No more tours. Those gigs just didn't pay well, but the outdoors is my home. You know that. I keep trying to get Rose to go rock-climbing. She says it's not her thing."

"Not yet," Avery noted.

"Not yet." He grinned with a long deep stare. She boldly met his gaze. An intense expression lined his face when he glanced up.

The beat of Avery's heart was strong in her chest. Thoughts about resuming her relationship with Jack had never been serious. Too much damage from the divorce and afterward had destroyed their foundation. But there was a spark, an undeniable connection they shared that was more than physical. *We had a life together,* Avery thought. *A child.*

The urge to reach out and grab his hand was strong.

"I'd like to talk about Rose," he said.

His demeanor had changed, along with his tone. More businesslike and disappointed. His hands were cupped before him and his back was straight. Slightly off-put by his sudden serious air, Avery leaned back and tried to act casual. The coffee and milk had arrived. Avery doused her coffee in sugar and creamer.

"What's up?" she asked.

"I heard you made a date with Rose and I tomorrow? A picnic? You're supposed to come and meet us at Northeastern?"

"That's right."

"I'd prefer if you didn't come," he flatly stated.

Avery nearly spit out her coffee.

"*What?*"

"Look," he mumbled and rubbed a hand through his hair. "I know you want to be a mom. You always have. You try, Avery. You really do. But being a mom has never really been your strong suit. I just think it's a mistake to lead Rose down that path again."

"I *am* a mom," Avery lashed out. "Did *you* carry her in your womb for nine months? Did *you* go through thirty-two hours of labor?"

"That's not what I meant," he said.

"What *do* you mean?"

"I'm talking about acting like a mom!" he complained. "You—trying to be a mom. Perfect case in point. Earlier today. You invited her over to help you unpack at your new place. *Great.* I loved that. Good job. But then, you completely vanished! *As always.* Did you forget about her? Because Rose certainly thinks you did.*"*

"Everything worked out fine," Avery said.

"In the end, sure," he replied, "and I was thankful for that. Rose had a great time, but before that, she couldn't get in touch with you for nearly forty minutes. She was driving around your neighborhood and freaking out. Finally she finds your apartment and you still don't pick up. You know who *does* pick up his phone? Me. *I'm* the one that has to deal with her when you decide you don't want to be a mom anymore. I've *always* been the one that picks up the pieces when you do or say something that breaks her heart."

Avery felt like she'd slipped into a horrible dream.

"I can't believe we're having this conversation," she said. "Rose and I had a great day today, and we're going to have a great day tomorrow."

"Are you sure?" he asked. "What happens if a call comes in? What happens if you have to cancel on her? What then?"

"Then we'll figure it out."

Jack laughed—a miserable, knowing laugh.

"See, *that's* what I'm talking about," he pointed out. "Listen to yourself. You're already making cancellation a possibility. Being a parent means you're there no matter what. When Rose is sick I take off from work. When she's depressed I sit by her side and hold her and talk to her. You can't just be a part-time mom."

"My life is complicated," Avery yelled. "I'm sorry if I don't have a steady job where I just sit behind a desk and draw pictures and answer phones. I can't just take off whenever I want. If a murderer is on the loose, I have to find them."

"What about when you were a lawyer? You never had time for Rose then either."

"If I remember correctly," Avery seethed, "you didn't have a job back then. I was the one paying the bills. *All the bills.* I'm sorry if I couldn't just take off whenever I wanted to be the perfect mother. How dare you," she hissed.

He sat back and shook his head.

"You haven't changed at all," he said. "I thought you were different. Rose swears you're different, but you haven't changed. You're still married to your work, just like you always were, and that means that one day—maybe not tomorrow or the next—but one day, you're going to let Rose down, *again*, and I'm tired of fixing your mistakes."

"You don't have to fix *anything* for me, Jack. We've been over for a long time."

"Rose," he said. "This isn't about me. It's about Rose."

Avery stood up and got in his face.

"Rose is a big girl now," she hissed. "She can take care of herself." A fake, menacing smile pulled at her lips as she stood tall.

"See you at the picnic," she said and walked out.

"Twelve o'clock," he called out after her. "*Sharp!*"

CHAPTER TWENTY ONE

Dammit! Avery thought.

It was stupid to meet with Jack after a long day, stupid to think things had changed and that maybe you could be a family again. Stupid! Ugh!

A light rain had begun to fall.

Fuming, all Avery could think about was the way Jack had set her up. *He never wanted to meet and just talk. All he wanted to do was lecture me. Why couldn't he do that on the phone? Why couldn't you see it?*

Dammit!

Mistake. It was a mistake. What other mistakes have you made?

The case came back to her. Venemeer, naked and positioned on a boat. Circle of friends and former employees. Desoto. Randall. The astrology professor.

She hopped in her car and called Ramirez.

His voicemail picked up.

Avery left a message.

"Hey, Dan," she said, "just wondering if you ran the rest of those names given you by Venemeer's contacts? Anyone have a record? Anything? Let me know."

Why didn't he answer? she wondered.

She sat in her car, listening to the pouring rain.

Ramirez doesn't have to tell you anything, she realized. *You're not an item. You practically told him as much. You alienated Dan, you just had a fight with Jack, and you can't stop thinking about this case.*

Dammit, she realized. *Jack is right. You're still married to your work.*

One of her former therapists had said the same thing: "Are you sure you aren't using work to escape from the world, Avery?" *Escape,* she thought, and she saw herself running through the woods trying to escape her father, and being beaten in a foster home to the screams of other children.

College life had been completely different, just like her law firm.

Carefree, she realized.

You were so carefree in college and working at Seymour & Finch, like you could do anything, be anything. You had it all together. You knew exactly where you were headed. To the exclusion of everyone else, she added. *Jack, Rose, anyone that came between you and your goals.*

She called Rose.

Her daughter picked up on the first ring.

"Hey, Mom. Good to hear from you. What's up?"

Avery watched the rain wash down her window.

"Nothing," she said. "I just wanted to hear your voice."

"You're not canceling tomorrow, are you?"

"Don't even think about it," Avery seethed.

"Excellent! Noon at the Back Bay Fens. By the war memorial?"

"I know."

"I'm excited!" Rose cheered. "OK, I've got to go now. A few of my friends are headed out to a party. See you tomorrow. I love you."

"I love you too."

The drive home was slow and miserable. Avery parked and used her jacket to protect her from the downpour as she ran into the building. The one bright side of the day was her new apartment. Even with the boxes and the darkness of night, the larger, brighter space made her feel like she could actually breathe. She pulled a beer from the refrigerator and stared at the rain through her balcony doors.

She imagined the killer, lurking in the darkness.

What are you *doing tonight?* she wondered.

After her beer, she nibbled on some leftovers and took a shower. The warm water cleared away much of her stress.

In bed, she put her computer on her lap and began to research astronomy.

Planets, stars, she thought. *What am I missing?*

Two hours later, she was fast asleep, the computer light shining in her face.

*

In her dreams, Avery was running. Monsters were behind her: Desoto, Randall, the boys from her orphanage. They crushed buildings and tore down walls. Avery moved in slow motion. Although she tried to run fast, her arms were like molasses, her legs took forever to rise and then touch the ground. The monsters were fast and relentless. Finally, they were upon her, all of them in a circle. Terror gripped her in that moment. None of them approached. Instead, they backed away to reveal a new terror, someone blanketed in shadow, with long black arms that reached down to grab her.

Avery shot up in bed.

"Huh!"

Her computer nearly fell to the floor, but in a quick motion, she jerked over to the side and grabbed it just in time.

Sunlight beamed through her windows.

Her phone was ringing: Dylan Connelly's cell.

She picked up.

"Hello?" she whispered and then cleared her throat. "Hello?"

"Avery," he said in a gentle voice that belied his gruff persona. "Sorry to wake you up. I know it's your day off. Captain said we can figure out how to make up the time to you later. Right now, we'd like you to come up to Lederman Park on the southern tip, just north of Longfellow Bridge. You know where that is?"

"Yeah," she said. "What happened?"

"There's another body."

CHAPTER TWENTY TWO

To get to the southern tip of Lederman Park, Avery had to take Embankment Road south along the park. As Longfellow Bridge drew closer, she could see that traffic had nearly come to a standstill heading east into Boston. Many people were out of their cars and pointing down toward the park. Similarly, two police boats were visible on the Charles River, close to the spot where she was headed.

The pointed tip of the park was dotted with shrubs and trees. Embankment Road turned onto a bike path. A state trooper vehicle was there, along with two police cars from the A1, an ambulance, forensics van, and photographer.

Dylan Connelly was easy to spot when Avery pulled up. His bulky chest and arms could barely fit into his gray jacket. He had thick blond hair that curled up in the front. The grimace on his face turned into a sigh at the sight of Avery, which surprised her. He'd been a miserable supervisor. Impossible to work with during her first big case as a detective, he was practically a ghost in the months that followed. Assignments simply appeared on her desk, or she was informed by the captain or Ramirez about an upcoming case; not at all like the Homicide supervisor he was supposed to be.

"Thanks for coming out," he said.

"I'm glad you called," she replied.

"Let me start by saying we're not sure this body has any connection to the marina. I would have handled it myself, but O'Malley wanted to loop you in because the body is in water. Maybe it's related; maybe it's not. Best you should be here to help figure it out."

"When was the body found?"

"About three hours ago."

"ID?"

"No clue yet."

He led her over a grassy strip toward the water. A tangle of bushes acted as a barrier. One spot of brush had been pulled apart in both directions, with the branches roped off by police to create a path.

"Forensics came through here first to make sure we wouldn't mess up the scene in case there was something to be found in the shrubs. They made a pathway afterwards. Randy is still down there with the body."

Randy Johnson was one of Avery's first friends when she arrived at the A1. The quirky forensics investigator had helped her on a few gang-related deaths during her rookie year, and had proved to be not only efficient, but fun.

On her hands and knees, one foot in the water and completely encased in branches and leaves, Randy held up a hand to keep Avery back. She wore standard field gear: white pants, white jacket, and a white shower cap to keep her hair back.

"Hold on, girl," she called. "Give me one more second."

The dead body was directly in front of Avery on the ground.

Half submerged in river, it was an older woman on her stomach: thin body, naked with a fan of gray hair around her head. Her legs drifted with the tide. Her torso was on a rock-and-dirt shelf. One of her hands was lost in the shrubs. Her right arm was by her side. No wounds were clearly visible. Hair was slightly parted toward the back of her neck, and Avery thought she could see a black-and-blue mark, possibly from strangulation.

Randy delicately lifted a lock of the woman's hair.

"Look here," she said.

The tiny red shirt of a child was visible beneath the hair.

"What is it?" Avery asked.

"One of many strange items around the body," Randy replied. "I'm just trying to figure out what might have been placed here, and what drifted in from the water. It's hard to tell. Look around. So far I've counted six suspicious items. See what you can find."

The area was by no means clean. Litter was scattered through the brush, and a plastic bottle was partially buried nearby. Focused on the outline of the body only, Avery cleared her mind and tried to imagine possible clues left by the killer.

A gold pin was visible. The label of something. She leaned down closer and noticed it was ingredients, maybe for peanut butter. There was also a husk of corn.

She repositioned herself to see areas of the body that weren't visible. Near the partially closed fist of the victim's left hand, Avery noticed a dangle bracelet and a loose piece of wheat.

The dangle bracelet lay in the dirt beneath the woman's hand, as if it had fallen there. It was grimy silver, with three items visible on it: a cross, a moon, and a heart.

A moon, Avery thought.

"I count six items as well," she relayed to Randy, "the child's shirt, a golden pin, corn husk, peanut butter label, dangle bracelet, and a piece of wheat. Is that what you got?"

"Give the girl a gold star!" Randy cheered. "I think we can discount the peanut butter label because that looks like it's been here for a long time. Maybe even the husk and the kid's shirt, which is really dirty."

"Agreed," Avery said. "I'm not sure about the pin. Not in line with the last kill. Not sure what a piece of wheat is doing here, either. That dangle bracelet attracted my attention. There's a moon on it. The killer might be some kind of astronomy nut. We're not sure. Was she wearing that, do you think? Holding it?"

"She was holding something," Randy said. "Might have fallen out of her grip."

"Why wouldn't the killer just put it on her wrist?"

Randy shrugged.

"What about the body?" Avery said. "Is this how you found it?"

"Exactly like this," Randy said. "Just floating, half in the water, half out."

Half in. Half out, Avery thought. *A woman and her shadow. Half and half. The new victim with part of her body on land, part on sea. What could it mean? What is he trying to say?*

"Can I see her face?" Avery asked.

"Sure."

Randy picked up a swath of hair and pulled it away.

The woman had a narrow neck, oval face, and a long nose. Avery guessed she was anywhere between forty and fifty. Strangely, the woman looked familiar. *Where have I seen that face before?* she wondered.

With no identification of the victim and little to go on by way of clues, Avery had to admit to Connelly that the dead body might not be related to her case. Still, she couldn't shake the moon amulet on the bracelet, or the feeling that she knew the victim.

Thompson and Jones were brought in to handle the area.

Avery watched as photographers took pictures and the corpse was eventually hauled out of the water and put into a black body bag.

She called Ramirez.

The phone went to voicemail.

"Hey," she said. "Where are you? Call me back."

Anger came to her then. She was angry. Angry at being ignored by Ramirez, angry at having no leads in her case, and angry at Randall for leading her down another empty path.

She checked the time.

It was still early. Ten o'clock.

One quick trip, she thought. *One quick trip and I'll be with Rose and Jack on a sunlit lawn in Northeastern and he'll see I love my family just as much as my work.*

CHAPTER TWENTY THREE

"You lied to me," Avery said.

Howard Randall sat before her. He looked healthier than the last time they'd met, almost as if her last visit had somehow rejuvenated his *joie de vivre*.

A frown came to him.

"Why would I lie?" he asked. "What do I have to gain, Avery? Is that why you came here? To force me to admit some kind of foul play?"

"*He gave you the cycle.* That's what you said. *'First body' doesn't necessarily refer to the victim.* You practically pointed me in the direction of astronomy."

A smirk came to his face.

"Did I? Are you sure? Because that's not how I see it at all."

"What is *that* supposed to mean?"

A menacing flair came to his nostrils. He pressed his palms on the table and leaned forward.

"*You know the rules!*"

"I'm not playing this game anymore."

"Then you'll get nothing," he snapped.

"Dammit!" Avery yelled.

"What do you think this is?" he asked. "You come in here every time you need help and I'm just supposed to give you whatever you need? I am in prison, Avery. I willingly offered to put myself in here, for *you*."

"Don't say that.

"For *you*," he stressed. "To help you, to show you the light. And what do you do? You act like a lost little girl. You come crawling in here for answers, *begging*," he said and pretended to cry as he spoke in the voice of a child, "because Detective Black really wants to do a great job! You're so predictable," he hissed in his own voice. "What a disappointment. Surprise me! Do something different. *Say* something different."

The way lay before her.

She could see it.

He wants information, she thought. *Give him information. Tell him about Rose, about your past, about everything. Get what you want.*

She couldn't do it.

The words wouldn't come out.

You're like a prostitute, she realized. *Ready to pimp out your life—your family.*

"I'm sorry," she said. "You're right. I *am* a disappointment. I don't know why I keep coming here. You know what I told my partner the other day? I said you were like a father figure to me. Can you believe that? That I would think—even for one second— that a murdering psychopath like you could possibly be my father?"

She laughed—bitter and hard.

Tears came to her eyes.

"Actually, I just realized something," she noticed. "That makes perfect sense. In a lot of ways, you're *exactly* like my father."

She stood up and banged on the door.

"Let me out of here!" she yelled.

"I guess, then, we're *both* disappointments," Randall whispered. "And for the record—cycles and bodies don't just refer to astronomy."

CHAPTER TWENTY FOUR

How can you break the cycle?
How can you take advantage of each moment in life?
I have found the key.
I can unlock the prize.
Come all who dare.
I defy you.
The first body is set. More will come.

Avery began to understand what he meant the moment Randall's door shut behind her. Instinctively, she turned back to gain more insight; the guard pushed her forward.

"Once you're out, you can't return," he said.

Astrology, she thought. *That has to be what he's been trying to tell me. Not astronomy, astrology.*

She recalled some of the lines from the letter. "How can you break the cycle? I have found the key. The first body is set. More will come."

He wants to change something, she realized, *something in his life. He thinks he can change it by using astrology. How is that possible?*

Avery had a basic layman's understanding of astrology. She knew it involved planets, and that each planet represented a sign. Where and when someone was born indicated their sign based on where the planets were during that time period. Some people even believed that a particular sign was like a lifelong badge that determined behavior patterns and personality traits.

I'm a Taurus, she thought. And she knew that because she was born in May, and apparently people born in May were in the sign of Taurus, which was supposed to mean she was reliable, patient, and stable. *Yeah,* she joked. *Patient and stable. That's me.*

Venemeer's bookstore, she realized.

For some reason, that had always remained in the back of her mind. Simms had been there. Ramirez had been there. But she'd never seen it for herself. There weren't any noticeable astrology books in Venemeer's apartment. *Why not?* she wondered. *If these killings are somehow related to astrology, there has to be evidence somewhere.*

Without a positive ID on victim number two, she hopped in her car and headed to her only possible lead: Venemeer's bookstore.

It was eleven thirty.

No way I can make that picnic, Avery thought.

Jack was right; you are *married to your work. That's not true!* she fought. *There's a killer on the loose. It's not like I need to answer emails or have some random phone conference. Every second I waste, someone could die!*

She dialed Rose.

The voice on the other end was tentative but hopeful.

"Hey, Mom. What's up? Where are you?"

A churning feeling crunched in Avery's stomach.

This sucks, she thought. *You're going to lose her again. I'm not going to lose my daughter over a goddamn picnic!* she inwardly fought.

"Rose, I've got some bad news. I can't make it. I know this is what you expected—and it's definitely what your father expected—but another body was found this morning and I just discovered a serious lead on the killer."

"No problem," Rose replied, flat and emotionless. "Thanks for calling."

Shit, Avery thought. *You've already lost her.*

"Honey, I swear, if it were anything else, I'd be there. This is too important. Someone's life might be at stake. Right now."

"Someone's life is always at stake, Mom. I feel like I've been hearing that for years. When you were a lawyer, it was about saving someone from a death sentence. Now it's about saving someone from a murderer. You know what I've learned in all that time? Life is about choices. You made yours a long time ago. Sorry I keep getting in the way."

The line went dead.

"Rose, that's not true. Rose!? Shit!"

You screwed up, Avery told herself. *Jack said you would screw up and he was right. How could I know about all this?* Avery fought. G*o to her, then. You can still make it. Say hello. Sit down for a few minutes. It's your day off. Do this later. For once, show your daughter you care.* Avery's mind screamed back: *There's a murderer on the loose!*

"Dammit!" she yelled aloud.

She ran a red light.

A car nearly smashed into her.

The driver turned and Avery turned her wheel at the last second and narrowly avoided a hit to her back end. Horns blared everywhere.

She pulled over to the curb.

The car she'd nearly collided with started up again and slowly inched away. Traffic resumed at the intersection.

Her heart was beating fast. Sweat dotted her face.

Two paths were laid out before her. On the one side, she saw Jack and Rose, laughing and drinking on a grassy lawn at a quiet university. On the other side, she imagined a killer stalking prey and ready to kill again. Memories flared: Her father stood over her with a shotgun. Edwin Peet's eyes shone yellow in the darkness as he hopped from side to side. The second victim, face down and naked in the Charles River.

I have no choice, she told herself. *I have no choice.*

She dialed Ramirez.

Again, he didn't pick up.

Avery left a message.

"I don't know why you're avoiding me," she said, "but there's a new body and I've got a lead. Meet me at Venemeer's shop on Sumner Street. I'm headed there now."

CHAPTER TWENTY FIVE

Venemeer's bookstore was called *Books for the Spirit*. The shop was bright and lined with windows that faced the street. Bookshelves littered the center and were only about five feet high. The bookshelves along the walls went from floor to ceiling. Each area of the shop was designated by a section: Reincarnation, Astronomy, Spirits & Ghosts, The Afterlife. There was even a children's section in the back, with age-appropriate spiritual books for kids.

Astrology had an entire bookshelf dedicated to it.

Avery picked up a book. The basics were easy to follow. The zodiac represented twelve constellations that lay across the sky. At the moment of birth, each of the planets in the sky, as well as the sun, occupied a certain position, and from those basic positions came the astrological signs. Her sign, she learned, Taurus, meant that the constellation of Taurus was behind the sun when she was born, which was why she was called a Taurus.

She gave a quick skim to every sign in the book.

At Gemini, Avery stopped. The symbol for Gemini looked like the Greek numeral for the number two, but the image depicted was either two women back-to-back, or the mirror image of one woman with a star in between them.

Avery felt hot.

Planets, she thought. *Cycles. The killer meant to leave a clue: the sign of Gemini. Why did he leave that sign? Was Venemeer a Gemini? Is it because Gemini depicts a woman? Did she die on some type of Gemini day? Find out,* Avery told herself.

Everything in the room became clearer, sharper. She scanned the four people in attendance and the clerk on duty before she returned to the book.

She looked at every other sign. Besides Gemini, only two other women appeared as symbols. Aquarius showed a woman with a jug of water. *Water*, she thought. *The second victim was found in the water.* The sign of Virgo depicted a woman with flowers in her hair. Avery discarded it. *There were no flowers at the scene.* No wheat or charm bracelet could be found in the images.

She perused one more book to confirm her theory. Sure enough, the Gemini symbol was the same; the others were similar to the first book.

Avery was angry and agitated.

Why did it take days *to figure this out?* she fought. *If I'd been on the case from the start, I would have made this connection earlier. I would have come to this bookstore on my own and talked to these people. Another death might have been avoided.*

Everyone in the store became a suspect.

The man behind the cash register was in his mid-thirties: black shaggy hair, dark circles under his eyes, and dressed like he was about to sleep in a garbage can rather than engage with customers. Hunched over and suspicious-looking. Avery's instincts told her he was no good. *On drugs,* she thought from his bloodshot eyes, *and keeping secrets.*

What else did the A7 miss? she continued to wonder. *What else?*

"Can I help you with something?" the clerk asked.

Avery flashed her badge.

"Detective Black," she said. "I'd like to ask you a few questions."

He rolled his eyes.

"If this is about Henrietta," he complained, "I already spoke to the police."

"I'm the lead investigator on the case," she replied. "You've never spoken to me. How long have you worked here?"

"I'm new," he lamented, completely bored. "Listen, I didn't really *like* Henrietta? I'm sad she's gone and all. We're not really sure what to do around here, but the manager, Martha Singleton? She's still at lunch. Maybe you'd like to wait for her."

He kept looking away, like he expected someone else to appear. Sweat began to form on his brow. He shifted his stance.

"What's your name?" Avery asked.

"Rick Bergen. I told you I'm new. I don't know anything."

"How long have you been here, Rick?"

"About four months."

"Are you nervous? You look a little nervous."

An angry glare met her gaze.

"Cops make me nervous," he said.

Sweat appeared under his armpits, on his neck. His face seemed to cry in sweat.

"Are you all right?" Avery asked.

Rick snapped.

"*I've got hyperhidrosis, all right!?* I sweat a lot. It's a thing. I take medication but it's obviously not working. Is that what you wanted to hear? You wanna embarrass me? *Fuck you, lady!* I have

96

rights too. How many cops are going to come in here and interrogate me? I haven't done anything wrong, all right?"

People were staring.

"Don't fucking look at me!" he demanded. "I'm going to file charges. I swear it. This is police brutality. I don't have to take this any longer!"

"Calm down, Rick," Avery whispered.

"You're making me nervous!"

"What do you have to be nervous about?"

He bit his nail and looked away.

"What size shoe do you wear?" Avery asked.

"My shoes? Why?"

"Just curious."

"Eleven. Is this a test or something? Are you going to tell me I'm an asshole because I wear size eleven shoes? I can't take this anymore!"

"All right, I'm back now. Everything's all right," someone said in a soothing voice.

A very tall woman with graying hair dyed black stood beside Avery. She was older, possibly the same age as Venemeer, with immaculate jewelry and wearing a knee-length yellow dress with colored circles. Avery had seen her picture in Venemeer's apartment.

"It's too much," Rick yelled. "I swear it!"

"I know, Rick. I know. This has been hard on everyone. Please, just calm down and I'll get to the bottom of this. Can I help you with something?" she asked Avery.

"My name is Detective Black," Avery said. "I'd like to ask some questions about Henrietta Venemeer. I know I'm not the first officer to come by, but I should be the last."

"That's fine, that's fine," she said. "Can we sit over there somewhere?"

"What's your name?"

"I'm Martha Singleton, the manager of the shop. Henrietta was a very dear friend of mine. I still don't quite believe it."

Avery glanced at Rick. He seemed to have calmed down. Although his face was red, the sweat was drying. He looked anywhere but at Avery. The people in the shop had already forgotten the incident and were back to reading.

Avery made a mental note to run Rick Bergen through the system, even though she was sure that Simms or Ramirez had already done it.

Martha led her to the children's section. She sat on a small couch and instructed Avery to sit on the windowsill so they could face each other.

"Don't mind Rick," she said. "He's very superstitious, and the police have been all over him about this terrible thing that's happened. He's not a criminal," she said and leaned forward to cup one side of her mouth. "It's just the pot. He smokes a lot of pot, you see. I think he's afraid the cops are going to bust him."

"I'm not interested in drug abuse," Avery said. "I'm looking for a killer."

Martha nodded with deep empathy.

"Well, I don't think Rick is a killer. He can barely keep the books straight."

"I notice you have a lot of astrology books here," Avery said. "Henrietta didn't have any in her home, at least none that I noticed. Any idea why?"

"Oh yes," Martha said. "She was *over* astrology. Henrietta went through phases, you see. This week might be doggie ghosts. Next week might be crystals. Astrology did not serve her well with her last boyfriend, so she refused to keep any in the house. We would have gotten rid of them in the shop but they're such big sellers."

"I believe you spoke with my partner. Daniel Ramirez?"

She thought for a moment.

"Oh yes," she said. "A very handsome gentleman."

"You mentioned there were a lot of people in her life that were strange or suspect in some way. Can you explain?"

"Well," she admitted, "Henrietta didn't have the greatest sense of self. She wasn't very confident, if you know what I mean? So anyone could express interest in her, or in the shop, and if they seemed halfway decent she allowed them into her life."

"Do you think any of them would have wanted to murder her?" Avery asked.

"No. I don't personally think the people I mentioned could commit murder. They were just odd, or overly aggressive at times."

"Like John Deluca."

"Yes." She brightened. "Like John. He's a perfect example. A very nice boy but strange, a little *off* somehow and he gets very angry."

"Did you mention that to my partner?"

Martha became very focused in that moment.

"No," she said, "and I regret that now. John Deluca wouldn't have committed murder. I'm not sure *any* of them would have. You see, I read a lot of detective novels. I know they're just novels," she said at Avery's smile, "but I consider myself a very good judge of people. I've been through some rough times in my life, and I think when you meet people that could commit a horrendous crime like murder, or *rape*," she emphasized with a slight stare and pause, "you realize there's something about them. It's not money or clothing or anything like that. It's something else. Something feels *off*. I've given this a lot of thought since I spoke with those other officers, and I realized something: Henrietta didn't always own this store. We've only been here for just over two years. She *worked* at a bookstore for a long time, an occult bookstore in South Boston. There was someone at the store that was always bothering her. I can't remember his name, but the store owner might. He's been there forever. His name is Mark Guzman. The shop is called Eye of Horus Bookstore. He might be able to help you more than I can."

"One more question," Avery said. "Do you happen to know Henrietta's sign? Her birth sign according to astrology?"

"Why yes," Martha said, "she was a Gemini."

CHAPTER TWENTY SIX

Avery tried to keep her excitement in check as she left the bookstore. She had just made a startling connection between the killer and his first victim: Henrietta Venemeer was a Gemini, and she'd been left to look like the sign of Gemini on a boat. But that was all Avery had. As gratifying as it was to know, she had no idea why.

Is he killing women for their astrological signs? she wondered. *What if he doesn't know them at all? What if it's just about their signs? No,* she thought. *That's not possible. He must be familiar with them somehow.*

Puzzle pieces with no form made her agitated and eager to act.

The Eye of Horus Bookstore was nearly impossible to find, a dark hole-in-the wall shop down a flight of stairs, stuffed between two large corporate buildings. On the way there, Avery had researched the owner, Mark Guzman. No record was on file.

After she parked, she made one more call to Ramirez.

The cop inside of her, the lead detective that expected her partner to be there whenever she needed, was upset that Ramirez hadn't called her back, but a part of her realized it was more than that. *He has a crush on you. He saved your life and he's been hitting on you since the day you met and finally you returned his advances and then you gave him the cold shoulder. Too bad!* she mentally snapped. *Regardless of whatever personal issues we may be going through, he's still my partner; he* has to *pick up.*

Ramirez answered on the third ring. The typical enthusiasm and childish glee was gone from his voice, replaced with a distant monotone.

"What's up?" he said.

"What do you mean 'what's up'?" she replied. "I've been calling you all day. Where have you been? We've got a lead."

"Yeah, I got your message."

"It's astrology," Avery continued. "The killer was trying to leave a message at the first body. The victim was placed that way like the sign of Gemini. The second victim might represent Aquarius. If she *was* a victim of our killer. One of Venemeer's friends gave me a lead. I'm out front at the Eye of Horus Bookstore, downtown. Can you get over here? I need my partner."

That last part hooked him in.

"I'll be there in a few." He sighed.

"What's wrong?" she demanded.

Silence for a moment.

"We'll talk soon," he said and hung up.

First Jack and now this, Avery thought. *That's all I need. Another talk.*

The bell jingled at the front door of the shop.

Inside, the bookstore was dark and tiny and cramped. There was barely enough room to walk down a single aisle. Rows of bookshelves branched off every ten feet on either side of the main pathway. Everywhere she looked, books were piled high. None of the titles appeared recent. They were old, mostly hardcover. One of the bindings read *Death Spells*. Avery ran her hand along another: *Witches' Brews*. As soon as she entered, the man behind a counter casually glanced up. He sat on a high stool behind a glass case filled with amulets and precious stones and all kinds of labeled bottles. Older, with graying hair on the sides, he wore reading glasses that slid down his face. A hawklike gaze penetrated Avery. A book was in his hands, and at the sight of her, he slapped it closed and leaned forward.

"Let me guess," he said. "You're a cop."

"How do you know?"

"The look of you." He frowned. "The cut of your clothes. Weren't always a cop though, were you? Probably someone of high standing. Maybe a bank manager, or a lawyer. Yeah, that's it." He snapped his fingers. "You were a lawyer."

"You're either psychic," she said, "or you read a lot of papers."

He threw out a limp wrist.

"I don't read any *papers*," he said. "What for? Same shit every day. Someone dies. Someone gets screwed. You want to know the *real* stories?" he asked. "All you have to do is look. You look at someone, gaze into their soul, see who they really are."

"Who am I?" Avery asked. "Really?"

He shrugged and appeared to lose interest.

"Everyone's different," he said. "And no one wants to hear the truth. They all want happy answers to make them feel good."

"*I* want the truth," she said.

"You?" he noted. "You look desperate, and lonely. Probably out on a case, no leads, and you showed up here because you've got nowhere else to go. How's that?"

Avery had to give him credit.

"Not bad," she said and flashed her badge. "Avery Black. Homicide detective."

A smile showed he was missing two teeth.

"I'm always right," he said. "It's a gift and a curse. What can I do for you?"

"Are you Mark Guzman, owner of this shop?"

"I am indeed the proprietor of this fine establishment," he said with a bow of his head.

"How long have you been here?"

"Almost twenty years, if you can believe that. Was here long before those two buildings crushed us like a sandwich. Construction was a nightmare when they went up. I thought it would be the death of me."

"Exactly what kind of shop is this?" Avery asked.

"You know," he said, "typical occult fare: voodoo, witchcraft, magic, black magic, devil worship, mysticism."

She glanced around.

"People really buy this stuff?"

"Oh yeah," he said. "Lots of people. Not here, though. Most of them don't come to the shop anymore. Ever since the Internet exploded, we have a great online business. People from all over the world find titles here. Rare books, translated texts, you name it."

A person appeared in the back. He was young, dark hair, wearing jeans and an AC/DC T-shirt. He glanced at Avery for a second. Surprise registered on his face and he quickly disappeared among one of the many stacks of books.

"Who was that?" Avery asked.

"Who?"

"That kid in the back."

"Oh, that's Dennis," he said. "Don't mind him. He's harmless. Comes in twice, three times a week to help me tidy up and keep the titles in order."

Something about him felt off to Avery.

"How long has he been working here?"

"About three months? Why?"

"He looked nervous."

"I bet," Guzman laughed. "A college kid at the tail end of puberty stuck in the stacks all day? Who knows what he does back there. Forget that. I don't want to know."

"I'm here because someone that used to work in your shop was recently killed. I was told you might be able to help. The victim's name was Henrietta Venemeer."

A hint of sadness crossed his face.

"Venemeer, huh?" he mumbled. "Too bad. Really, too bad. We weren't friends. I'll be honest. But it's sad to see anyone go. The older you get, the more you realize life is about those connections you make. Once they're gone, what do you really have?"

"How long did she work here?"

"About four, five years?"

"But you weren't friends?"

"No, not at all," he easily stated. "Henrietta could be a real jerk, if you want to know the truth of it. Very bossy. Always had to be her way. The reason I kept her around was because she was the best bookkeeper I ever met. Amazing with the accounts. She majored in business, I think, but she loved books. Worked at a publishing house for a while, decided she wanted something a bit more family-oriented. Savages over there in publishing. Everything is about formula. Here," he signaled to the shop, "it's all about the books."

"Did she ever have problems with anyone?"

"Problems? Henrietta? She had problems with everyone." He laughed. "Sorry." He quickly recovered. "That's not funny. We need to have respect for the dead. Sorry, Henrietta," he said to the sky. "But it's true," he added to Avery. "She rubbed people the wrong way. It was never about the customer, it was always about the books. For example, someone would come in but they wouldn't know anything about the title they wanted because it was a gift. Well, right then and there, Henrietta wrote them off. They weren't *book* people, she'd think."

Avery tried to keep him focused.

"Anyone in particular?" she said. "Someone she might have upset? This person is most likely a man, very well versed in astrology, strong, and angry."

He lowered his chin and eyed Avery from above his glasses.

"This is an occult bookstore," he said. "Crazy comes with the territory."

"Someone was murdered," Avery said. "Try to keep some perspective. I'm looking for a man capable of murder that had a relationship with Henrietta Venemeer and possibly worked in this shop or came into this shop often."

He thought about it for a moment.

"You know?" he realized. "I've got a customer that used to come in here all the time—still does occasionally—and he hated Henrietta. He worshiped black magic, astrology, voodoo, all of that stuff, and said he was going to make sure she paid for her insults. Creepy guy. Even by my standards."

"You didn't think that might have been relevant information for the police?"

"For what?" he cried. "People make idle threats all the time. Henrietta didn't care. If I put out an APB for every voodoo witch doctor that wanted to stick pins in my side, I'd be out of business."

"What's this guy's name?"

"Harold Bowler. Lives in one of those fancy houses on Columbia Road, right by the water. Very rich. And very, very strange. Venemeer wasn't the only one he hated, either. He's one of those guys that has so much money, it warps their mind. They begin to think they're gods or something, and that they can do anything."

"Anyone else come to mind?" Avery asked.

"Nah, that's it," he said and pointed to a necklace in his case. "Want a protection charm?"

Avery patted her gun.

"I've got all the protection I need."

CHAPTER TWENTY SEVEN

Avery sat in her car, door open and one leg out, while she researched Harold Bowler. Sure enough, he was in the system: six unanswered speeding tickets, a DUI, aggravated assault, animal cruelty, public nuisance, public indecency, and endangering the life of a minor, which was filed by his own brother.

That's some rap sheet for a millionaire, Avery thought.

His DUI arrest showed the picture of a cocky, thickset man, possibly in his late thirties or early forties, with recently cut brown hair and an impervious stare that reminded Avery of hedge fund managers and multimillionaires that weren't afraid of anything, including the law.

Ramirez walked up to the car just as Avery was about to close the door.

"Where are you parked?" she asked.

"Just down the street." He pointed.

"Get in, I'll drive."

He seemed hesitant.

"What's *with* you?" Avery demanded. "There's a lot going on right now and I need my partner. Is this about your day off or something, because I'm off too."

"It's nothing like that." He waved it off.

"Then what is it?"

An unkempt air surrounded Ramirez. He still had the bruises from his fight with Desoto. His hair was frizzed without gel. The slacks he wore lacked a certain sharpness.

"Last run for you and I," he said.

"What's that supposed to mean?"

"I don't want you as my partner anymore," he said and gave her a long, hard stare right in the eyes. "I already talked to O'Malley."

Avery stood up.

"What? *Why?*"

"You!" he shouted. "It's always about you. Whatever Avery wants, Avery gets. You're the best shot. You figure everything out. You take on five guys with no problem—"

"Is that what this is about? I can fight better than you?"

"*I don't care about your fighting*," he said. "I like you—a lot! How many times do I have to say that? But you don't care about *me*, and you sure as hell don't need me on the job. I thought we had something," he lamented. "And I want more than this, but it's too

105

confusing. Every time you call, I'm not sure if you're calling for *me*, because you miss me and want to see me, or if you're just calling about the job. By the way, it's *always* about the job."

"Dan," she said.

"No. Don't do that. It's over. I already asked for another assignment. I'm here because I wanted to tell you in person."

The revelation was a shock for Avery. She never thought Ramirez cared so deeply. *No*, she instantly argued. *That's a lie. You knew he wanted more, you just weren't ready to give it, so you played both sides and now you got burned.*

"We have a lead," she said. "You want to come along?"

Ramirez laughed.

"You see? You're incredible, really. I just poured my heart out to you. I'm hurting. This hurts me," he said and pounded on his chest, "and that's the first thing you say to me?"

She wanted to say more.

She wanted to shout: *I do care! I want you to hold me and make me feel like I'm a part of something bigger than criminals and dead bodies!* But she couldn't. A killer was out there, waiting. Time kept ticking by, and she was standing in the street having an argument with someone when lives were at stake.

"I'm really screwed up, aren't I?" she said.

"You are!" He laughed. "Thank you for recognizing that."

"I'm going to work on this," she said. "I promise. I'll fix this. Right now, though, can we just put this on hold for a second and track down a lead?"

Ramirez breathed out a sigh.

"Sure," he said. "Why not? One last ride."

CHAPTER TWENTY EIGHT

Tension was thick in the car as Avery drove the two of them to the coast. Ramirez had his head turned for most of the way.

"You hear about the latest victim?" she said.

"That woman could be anybody." Ramirez shrugged.

"What did you hear?"

"Still no positive ID. Prints weren't helpful. They're sending her picture around."

"So you've been working all day," she noted. "Doing what?"

"Doing my job!" Ramirez said and faced her. "What do you mean 'doing what'? I care about this job just as much as you, Avery. The difference is, I know when to turn it off and on. You have no off switch. You're *always* on. Were you on when you kissed me? What about when we held hands and stared into each other's eyes? Was that all to make me a more dedicated partner or something?"

"Of course not! I can't believe you think that."

"I don't know *what* to think," he snapped.

A few minutes later he resumed the conversation.

"I followed a bunch of dead leads I got from Venemeer's friends. On my own," he stated with a grudge, "just like you. Guess I'm picking up *all* your habits."

Avery refused to get into another argument, especially with a man she wasn't even dating who was *supposed* to be her Homicide partner.

Harold Bowler's house was a red three-story colonial mansion in white trim that overlooked the beach. Groomed shrubbery surrounded a grass lawn.

Avery parked out front.

"This guy's got a lot of citations, including aggravated assault. I'll need some backup on this one. Are you with me?"

"I'm right here," Ramirez complained without meeting her gaze.

Two cars were parked in the driveway: a sleek, black Mercedes sports car and an old but brilliantly remodeled red Mustang convertible.

"Look's like he's home," Avery said.

Up a set of white stairs to the front door, Avery could clearly see the lawn. A post was planted in the lawn's center. Most of the grass had been eaten away, and there were droppings everywhere.

"That doesn't look like dog poop," Ramirez noted.

"How do you know *that*?"

"It just doesn't. Look at it. Does that look like dog poop to you?"

A strange chant was coming from inside the house, loud enough to be heard from the porch. Avery peeked into a few windows and saw nothing.

She rang the bell.

Nothing changed. The music continued and no one answered.

She pushed the bell again. The front door was locked. She gave Ramirez a look and pointed around the house. They each went their separate ways. Avery moved into the shrubs and over the mangled lawn. First-floor windows were too high to peek through. Basements were nonexistent since the house was so close to the ocean. Two of the second-story windows she saw were blacked out. She met Ramirez at the back door, which was also locked. The music continued to pound, a tribal chant of some kind.

Avery glanced around the neighborhood and then quickly thrust her elbow into one of the small windows on the back door. Glass shattered.

"Hey," Ramirez said. "What are you doing?"

Avery shrugged.

"The door was broke. We thought it was a robbery and went in to investigate."

He shook his head.

"Great. Now we're felons."

Music hit her when she stepped inside.

"Hello?" she called. "Is anyone home? Harold Bowler? Are you in here? Your door was broken and unlocked. Are you all right?"

The expansive kitchen could have fit fifty people. A grand piano stood in the living room. Everything in the house was bare, with minimal furniture and polished wooden floors. Bookshelves were everywhere and filled with bound texts on everything from magic to religion. Avery and Ramirez checked every room and closet. Lots of masks, tribal gear, and clothing, but no weapons, and nothing astrological.

A set of stairs to the second floor. Avery unholstered her gun.

"Windows were blacked out up top," she whispered to Ramirez.

"*Harold Bowler!?*" she called out. "*This is the police. Are you in here?*"

Stomping noises sounded above the music, and an animal cry of some kind.

Avery picked up her pace.

Gun low, she reached the second level and turned. There were multiple white doors and a long hallway that branched off in two directions. One of the doors was shut; underneath was darkness and sporadic flashes of light. The music pounded even louder.

Ramirez checked the other rooms and closets while Avery kept watch on the dark room from which the noise emanated. When Ramirez returned, he shook his head.

Behind the questionable door, a man's voice cried out. The words were violent and unintelligible. An animal's cry turned into a gurgle and silence. More screams came from the man above an eerie African beat.

Avery put her back against one side of the door. Ramirez mirrored her position on the other side. Both had their guns out and high. Ramirez gave her a nod.

Avery turned the doorknob and thrust it open.

"*Police*," she cried.

The dark room was only lit by lava lamps, four of them, one in every corner, each a different color: pink, green, yellow, and blue. No furniture was anywhere, only blankets. The walls were littered with masks and symbols written in what appeared to be blood.

On his knees, and with a large knife in his hands, was Harold Bowler. Shocked at being discovered, he moved his gaze from Avery and Ramirez to the large, dead goat that lay before him, throat slit and oozing blood.

Ramirez moved around the room and turned off the electronics. Music was silenced.

Avery flicked on the light.

Bowler's initial surprise at the intrusion turned to outrage.

"*What the hell are you doing in here?*" he yelled.

Unabashed at his naked form, he stood up and pointed the weapon at Avery.

"You're in a lot of trouble, lady."

Avery flashed her badge.

"We're police," she said. "We heard screams coming from your house. The door was busted so we came in. What are you doing?"

"This is private property," he said. "I can do whatever the hell I want."

"Is this some kind of ceremony?" Ramirez asked.

"*Get the hell out of my house!*"

"We need to talk," Avery said. "*Now*. Put on some clothes."

Bowler threw the bloody knife to the ground. In a sentimental moment, he lowered to his knees, kissed the dead goat, and whispered in another language.

"What did you just say?" Avery asked.

"*Fuck you*," he snapped.

As Bowler grabbed a shirt and underwear, he said: "What's your name? Detective Black? *Black?* I know you. You're that cop from the papers, right? Well, let me tell you what tomorrow's headline is going to read: *Hero Cop Fired for Breaking And Entering.* How does that sound, Black?"

Bowler led them into another room with a bed and a lounge chair.

He doesn't limp, Avery noticed.

He slumped into the lounge and threw up his hands.

"What could this possibly be about?" he demanded. "Is this about those speeding tickets? Chump change. I don't have *time* for that, you understand? You want some money? There's tons of money in that top dresser drawer over there. Take it and leave. You just screwed up about a month of preparation. But I guess you wouldn't know anything about that, would you?"

"What were you just doing?" Avery asked.

"I'm a *Bokor*," he said with pride and tapped his chest, "a voodoo priest with very heightened spiritual powers. That goat in there is Fanny. The ceremony was designed to destroy my financial competitors and bring a new wave of wealth to my technology sector, which could use all the help it can get. The gods are going to be pissed now. I could sue you, you know that? Let me think about how much I stand to lose because of your stupidity."

He tapped on his chin and pretended to think.

"This is crazy," Ramirez said. "He's in his house killing a goat, and he wants to sue us."

"*In his house*," he cried. "Those are the relevant words. I'm *in my house*. No nuisance laws are being broken. I don't intend to sell Fanny to any hungry hobos. No animal cruelty is happening here. She was killed quickly, *in my own house*, for the purposes of a religious ceremony. The only ones breaking the law right now are you two."

"Harold Bowler," Avery said, "are you familiar with the death of Henrietta Venemeer?"

He laughed.

"Yeah, I'm familiar with it," he said. "Too little, too late, as far as I'm concerned. I was trying to get that bitch killed for years.

Used some of my most powerful magic. But I was a novice back then," he admitted. "Made a lot of mistakes. What about it?"

Avery's heart quickened.

"You knew her?"

"Yeah, I knew her. I had to deal with her every time I wanted a book. Like dealing with the Gestapo. Made me feel like an idiot half the time. I hated her. Good riddance. Why are you here? Are you here because of Venemeer?" He laughed again. "That's a good one. You think I killed her or something?"

"Where were you on the night of the murder?" Avery asked.

"Oh man, this is priceless." He smiled. "You do think I killed her! You must really need some help on this one, don't you? To come to *me*, of all people. I don't give a shit about Venemeer. All that was years ago. I don't carry grudges. I live in the moment. I can account for myself every night this week," he said and rambled off a number of the best restaurants in Boston. "You ever have the quail dish at DuPovre's? No. Of course not," he said. "That would cost more than your weekly salary."

He kicked his legs up onto the armrest.

The bottom of his feet were bare and caked in dried blood. And they were small.

Eight and a half, Avery realized. *Nine, tops.*

He's not our guy.

She could easily assess that Harold Bowler was a jerk: he practically bribed them to leave, and he must have been violating *some* kind of laws with a dead goat in his house, but Avery had no idea which ones. Regardless of his actions, he had no limp, his shoe size didn't match up, and he felt all wrong for Venemeer. She tried to ease out of the situation with as much dignity as possible.

"We came by your house to discuss a murder case," she noted. "We saw your door downstairs had a broken window—"

"Oh, that's great. So you broke my window, too?"

"We heard screaming," Avery continued. "We thought there might be a robbery taking place, so my partner and I headed into your house. No one answered our calls. You're obviously not the person we're looking for."

"Yeah, but I'm looking for *you* now, Black," he said with one eye closed and a finger pointed at Avery. "You're right in my line of sight."

CHAPTER TWENTY NINE

Lost among the crowds at the New England Aquarium in Central Wharf, he felt out of place and more alone than when he was by himself. He moved through a glass tunnel and gazed around at all the fish and sea creatures in the glistening blue water above his head.

Children screamed around him and parents pointed.

He lost sight of his victim often. There was no real need to keep track of her. She was on a blind date and taking her time, and his journey was all about patience, and timing.

In one of the aquarium rooms, a large, shallow pool had been created where people could touch stingrays. His victim was having the time of her life. She was young, only in her late twenties, very pretty with dark brown hair and hazel eyes. Her date splashed water on her. She grabbed him and laughed. He couldn't laugh. In fact, the scene made him angry, so angry that the red visions appeared again, and he was forced to put his face in a wall and take in the slow, timed breathing he'd learned in a meditation class.

Relax, he whispered in his mental mantra.

He flashed on a memory of the girl. Her mouth was flat and her eyes held only disdain and impatience. All he'd wanted was help, and guidance. What did he get? A rote answer and a hand that waved him to another line. *She was the problem,* he thought. *Not me. Now she's going to help me solve everything.*

In room after room, he tried to enjoy himself. If he'd learned anything from the wait before a kill, it was that joy in his surroundings produced calm, and calm allowed the time to go by much, much quicker. The penguins appealed to him, as did the jellyfish tank.

A loudspeaker came on.

"Ten minutes. The aquarium will close in ten minutes."

After the closing, he followed the happy couple to a restaurant nearby. He'd been watching her for nearly two months, in tandem with all of the other women he intended to utilize in his plan. He was surprised at how easily she was enamored with her date. The man obviously had no interest in her; he only lit up when she looked at him, and every chance given he went in for a hug or kiss. *He wants to use her,* he thought. *Just like me.*

He found a quick bite at a local deli near the restaurant. After he ate, he took one more look at the happy couple and then moved onto his next location.

He drove a beat-up blue Cadillac that he'd bought from a friend. The engine sounded like it popped every time he turned it on, and smoke always sputtered from the exhaust pipe. The drive was slow, and he imagined it was like the universe in his mind, the turning planets and the alignment up above that was soon to come.

On the seat next to him was a newspaper from the night after his first kill. The paper was turned to the interior article on the crime scene. A single name was circled: Avery Black. *She thinks she can stop me?* he wondered. *She'll help me. She'll be part of it.*

He drove to a nice house in South Boston where the young girl rented out the basement apartment of an elderly couple. The apartment had two entrances: a private entrance was available in the backyard, but someone could also enter from the basement door.

As was his custom, he parked a few blocks away and walked back to his destination. He took in the lovely houses around him, the trees and night sky. No harm could come to him on this night or any other. Long ago, he had made a pact with the moon, and whenever that great celestial body moved through a particular astrological sign, that's when he worked, and that's when he was safest.

A dog barked in the neighboring house as he reached the back door to the young victim's basement. The tools in his hands were easy to maneuver through the thin black gloves that he wore. He jimmied the lock open. He checked the latch to ensure it would work, slipped inside the darkened room, and closed the door behind him.

At approximately eleven thirty, he heard laughter from outside.

The girl appeared in the door's window. She kissed the boy. He pulled her close and wanted more. She turned away. "Not tonight," she said. "I had a great time. Call me?" He swore he would call. She kissed him again and turned into the apartment.

The light switch wouldn't work.

"Everything all right?" he called.

"Yeah, just the lights," she said. "I'm sure it's an easy fix. See you later."

She closed the door behind her.

And as she groped for the electricity box, he stood up from his chair.

He walked toward her.

And he reached out.

CHAPTER THIRTY

The next morning, Avery awoke with a feeling of anxiety, stress, and loneliness. Everything in her life seemed like it was a mess. Rose refused to answer her calls, Ramirez barely talked to her after the animal-sacrifice affair, she had no more leads, and worst of all, it was an official work day, which meant she had to head to the office.

She'd only had one drink the night before, and she'd gone to bed relatively early, but Avery felt like she was hungover. A pair of sunglasses hid her bloodshot eyes. She pulled a black blazer over a blue shirt.

The person that stared back at her in the mirror, despite the glamorous makeover, appeared just as tired and depressed.

Great, Avery thought. *The perfect start to the day.*

The A1 was bustling with action that morning, a spill-over from the night before: rowdy college kids and strippers.

"Hey look," a cop joked. "It's Avery Black, movie star."

Avery waved and took off the shades.

On the second floor of the department, people were already deep in whatever case they were on. Cops yelled into phones and poured over case files.

"Black! Get in here. *Now!*" she heard.

O'Malley waved her into his office. At the same time, Connelly made an exit and gave Avery a look that was both apologetic and curious.

What's wrong with that guy? she wondered.

"What's up, boss?" she said.

"*Connelly's* your boss," O'Malley pointed out. "I'm the captain. Get it straight."

"Ouch," she whispered.

"Yeah, *ouch*," he echoed. "That's exactly how I feel right now. Sit down."

O'Malley needed a new dye job; the gray was starting to show at his roots. He wore a red plaid shirt that seemed more suited to a lumberjack. It was very out of character; he usually wore suits to work.

"Nice shirt," Avery said.

He settled into his desk, hands steepled, and leaned forward.

"What is it with you, Black? I can't figure you out. One minute, I think you're a genius. The next minute? I think you're an idiot. Which one is it?"

"My ex-husband would tell you I'm a little of both."

He sighed.

"Well, we've got a lot to discuss. First off, we've got a new letter. This one was mailed directly to you."

"To *me*?"

"Came in late last night. Was put on a police cruiser window under the wipers. Had your name on the envelope: *To Avery Black*. Cop opens it up, sees a bunch of gibberish but knows it might be important so he sends it around. We got it at about six. So did the local papers. This is a copy. Forensics still has the original. So far, nothing."

Avery picked up the copied sheet of paper. It was handwritten in the same scratchy penmanship as the last.

Avery Black.
Sadly, I have no use for you.
What a powerful planet you'd make.
I don't like being tracked.
Want to find me?
Sun: Sagittarius: fifteen degrees fifty-nine
Moon: Scorpio: seventeen degrees twenty-seven
Ascendant Libra: sixteen degrees fifty-nine

"What does it mean?" Avery said.

"The paper says it's astrology," O'Malley replied and handed her the morning edition.

Sure enough, a blown-up portion of the letter was once again on the front page, along with a picture of Avery from her rookie days. The title read: *Astrological Killer Issues a Warning*. The article inside went on to discuss how the sun was the major astrological sign which indicated someone's birth, while the moon and the ascendant were two planets that also had major effects on that birth. But without further information, the paper said the coordinates were practically useless.

"Why would the killer give us useless information?" Avery asked. "I've been reading about natal charts. They show where all the planets are located when we're born. You just need a birthdate, time, and place of birth."

"We know all that," O'Malley said. "Thompson said these coordinates happen a lot, so if you put them in a chart they would just give you a lot of different times and dates. You need everything else to make an accurate prediction—where all the planets were.

Yeah, I know." He nodded. "Who knew Thompson was an astrology nut?"

Avery scoured the letter.

"It has to mean *something*," she said.

"We also identified that second body," O'Malley added. "Connelly and Jones were handling it, but now they're pretty sure it might be yours. She was an astronomy professor at the Observatory. Retired about five years ago."

Avery's heart quickened.

"We were just at the Observatory," Avery said.

"I know. This might be your lead. Thompson has been on the phone all morning with the university. He's trying to find out every student that went through her doors in the last ten years. Might take a while, but that's all he's doing."

"Why Thompson?"

"Ramirez is no longer your partner."

"*What?*"

Although she knew Ramirez wanted to take a break from their partnership, after the animal-sacrifice debacle the night before, she assumed he'd gotten over it.

"That can't be a shock," O'Malley delicately whispered. "He said he was going to talk to you about it, right?"

"He did."

"Well?"

"I just—I didn't think he'd actually go through with it."

"You can't play with people like that, Avery. Ramirez is a very delicate guy. He fell for you, hard from what I can see. You can't give and then take, give and then take," he said with an uneven balance of his open palms, "especially when you work with someone. Don't shit where you eat, right? You've never heard that expression?"

"I've heard it," she said.

"Well, you should start *abiding* by it. Like it's law."

"Thompson?" she asked.

"You two worked well together on the Peet case, no? You blew him off in the end, sure, but you won't do that again, right?" he asked with a very intense gaze. "Besides, he's not on anything right now. Finley will partner with Ramirez to finish your backload while you focus on this case exclusively. The clock is ticking, Avery. The mayor called me yesterday. Wanted an update. What am I going to tell him?"

Avery was having a hard time absorbing what she'd already heard. Ramirez had pulled the trigger. He was out. *I must have hurt him bad,* she realized. *How am I going to make this up to him?* Other thoughts invaded her mind: The second victim was an astrology professor.

"Her birthday," Avery said.

"Huh?"

She looked up.

"The second victim. What was her birthday?"

"Why?"

"*What was it?*"

O'Malley flipped through a file on his desk.

"Her name was Catherine Williams. Born September fifteenth."

September fifteenth, she thought. *That has to be Aquarius. It has to be. Water. She was found near water.* Avery plugged the date into her phone and asked for the corresponding zodiac sign. Her body deflated at the answer: Virgo. *Virgo?* she fought. The only two pictures of Virgos she'd seen had women dancing or with flowers in their hair. *What am I missing?*

"What are you doing over there?" O'Malley said.

"Nothing, sorry."

"Here's the file on Williams," he said and handed it over. "Connelly and Finley were at her apartment this morning. Very similar to the first victim. Cameras disabled. No sign of forced entry into the apartment, so he either knew her or knew her schedule. Nothing missing from what they could tell, not even a rug. Phone and email don't show any signs to a possible abduction or kill. How the hell is this guy getting those bodies out of the apartment without a single person seeing them?" he wondered.

"Garbage bags," Avery said.

"What?"

Her mind was working too fast to stop.

"We should also have Thompson compile a list of all the people employed by Venemeer's shop," Avery said, "or the occult bookstore she worked at before branching off on her own. That might help pinpoint a name."

"Good. Tell him on the way out. What do you mean by garbage bags?"

Avery shook her head.

"Something I learned as a rookie. Best way to get a body around unnoticed is to pretend you're someone that *supposed* to handle large objects, like a sanitation worker or a mover. He took the first victim out in a rug, right? And no one seemed to think about it twice. He might have been wearing a disguise for the second victim too. Did they ask any witnesses about that? A large worker moving heavy items?"

"Find out."

Avery stood to leave.

"Sit down," O'Malley said.

She sat down.

"One more thing," he mumbled. "And you're not going to like it."

"I don't like *any* of this," she shot back.

"You need to see a psychologist. Court ordered. You start today."

"What? *Why?*"

A sad look was in his eyes.

"Really? You don't know?"

"Is this about Randall?" she fought. "OK, sure. I went to see him again. So what? He *helped* me. He gave me the astrology lead."

"Randall? I don't know anything about that. Listen, you want to keep that psycho in your life, that's your call. You know what I *do* care about? People calling this department and demanding your resignation. That's right," he said, "*your resignation.* Do these names sound familiar?" He picked up a piece of paper on his desk. "Rick Bergen?"

"I just asked him a few questions. Is it my fault that he sweats a lot?"

"Harold Bowler?"

Avery raised her brows.

"Now that guy is crazy," she noted. "Have you seen his rap sheet? *He was in the middle of an animal sacrifice!*"

"I don't care if he was in the middle of a mass murder! You broke into his house—"

"That window was busted!"

He waved her lies away.

"You broke into his house with no warrant and no probable cause. You can't just go around and do whatever you please, Avery. You give this department a bad name, and word spreads and it all comes down to me. You've got no leads on this case, you've been wasting my time, you've been getting angry, and you're taking your anger out on innocent people. *That's* unacceptable, and *that's* why you're going to see a shrink."

"Please don't make me see a shrink."

"It's either that, or you're off the case. What do you want?"

Without a word, Avery sat back and crossed her arms.

"That's what I was hoping you would say." He nodded. "You'll see Sloane Miller, our resident psychologist. She's got an office downstairs. Maybe you've seen her before?"

"No," she said.

"You've got the file. Thompson is already working hard. Give him the update about the bookshops. The second body is with the coroner if you want to see that for yourself. That letter was sent to everybody so you might want to check other papers and the Internet. Maybe they know something we don't."

He leaned forward.

"Tread lightly, Avery. You're on thin ice right now."

CHAPTER THIRTY ONE

The office of Sloane Miller was tucked away down a long hallway on the first floor. Avery knocked and instantly prepared to leave when someone called out: "Hold on a sec!"

Shrinks were nothing new to Avery. She consulted a revolving door of psychologists and therapists and analysts over the years: first after her father was sent to prison, then during the worst years of her life when she was forced to leave Seymour & Finch. Some of their wordage was still in her mind. "You have to open up, Avery." "Relax a little. Have you ever been on a vacation?" "What makes you happy? *Really* happy?"

I am not going to see a shrink, she thought.

The door opened to reveal a small room with only enough space for two or three people. Sloane had a desk and a chair. There was one extra chair and a long couch on the wall closest to Avery.

Sloane's age was hard to guess. *Late thirties?* Avery wondered. *Early forties?* The psychologist had a warm, loving glow about her: bobbed brown hair, blue eyes, and wearing a nice dress with stockings.

"Hi there," she said with a smile.

Avery mentally groaned and turned around.

"Oh, please don't go," Sloane called. "I do that sometimes. Mothering. My tone is very mothering, isn't it? My friends say it's because I don't have any children of my own. Sometimes I have to remember that. I apologize."

Against the door frame, Avery leaned into the office with half her body in the hall.

"You're Avery Black, aren't you?" Sloane said.

Avery nodded.

"It's nice to finally meet you," Sloane said. "You've been in the papers so much lately I feel like I know you. Well, the part of you the papers write about," she corrected with a knowing grin. A hand tapped on the couch. "Would you like to sit down? I have a half hour free."

Uncomfortable to the tenth degree but lulled into the office by Sloan's gentle manner, Avery rolled into the room and plopped down on the couch.

"Your body language tells me you really don't want to be here," Sloane said. "I'll try to make this as painless as possible," she whispered.

Her words and tone reminded Avery of a wise old lady that had accrued a lifetime of experience, so it was a surprise to constantly view her and see a perky young woman.

"Let's see here," Sloane said and faced her desk. "Avery Black. They got a court order to see me. That's impressive."

"What does that mean?"

"Oh, it just means someone wants to cover their butts," she said. "Usually there's been a complaint about an officer, and the department has a court-issued session or two to show that they're complying, in case that same person calls again. Is that what happened?" Sloane asked and turned around. "Did someone complain about you?"

"Yeah," Avery said. "Multiple people."

"Were their reasons valid?" she asked.

"Maybe," Avery thought. "Sometimes I get so involved in a case that I lose perspective. Everyone starts to look like a criminal."

"That makes a lot of sense," Sloane agreed. "I treat a lot of police officers and I can tell you this is a common issue. You never know who's holding a gun, or who could be a killer in a room of hundreds. People are always quick to talk about police brutality or racism, but I've learned firsthand what you go through."

Avery was waiting for the ax to fall. For the big questions to come. For the accusations to fly. She wasn't prepared for such a normal, everyday discussion.

"You're not like other shrinks I've seen," she said.

"Have you seen many?"

"A few."

"What were your issues? Why did you go see them?"

"Different issues for different times." Avery shrugged. "Depression. Alcohol abuse. Once, I wanted to get my daughter back and I wasn't sure how, so I just went to talk and figure it out. You name it and I've probably needed the help."

Sloane picked up a pad and pencil to take notes.

"Why are you here now?" she asked.

"I was told I had to come."

Sloane laughed and covered her mouth.

"I'm sorry about that," she said. "I know we've only just met, but I find it hard to believe someone can make you do *anything* you didn't want to do. Let me rephrase that. Why did you choose to enter my office just now?"

"Captain said I'm either off my current case or I come here. And I don't want to be off my case. If you've been reading the papers lately, you know why."

"You're very dedicated, aren't you?"

"*I* think so."

"That's an admirable quality. Dedication usually means you're loyal, courageous, and persistent. However, like all things, it can be good *and* bad. You said before that sometimes you get so involved in a case that you lose perspective. Have you noticed any other ways that being too dedicated has hurt you, instead of helped you?"

Jack's words rang out in her mind: *You're still married to your work, just like you always were.* And Avery recalled the collapse of her family, during a time in her life when she thought everything had been going her way.

"I've always been so dedicated to my job that everything else seemed to fall away: relationships, family, friends."

"Would you like those things in your life?" Sloane asked.

Avery faced her.

"Yeah," she honestly replied. "I would."

"Is there *room* in your life for those things?"

That question was harder for her to answer. On the face of it, there was lots of room: a spacious apartment to meet with family and friends, time when she had off work. But in her mind, she was a closed shell, a constantly churning machine trying to find answers and solve riddles, and in that machine, there was no room for anyone.

"You look upset," Sloane said. "What's going on? Talk to me."

Suddenly, Avery understood.

Work is your life. Everyone knows it but you.

The jarring realization suffocated Avery. She felt stifled by everything: the office, her own clothing and life. She stood up to leave.

"Sorry," she said. "I've got to go."

"What's wrong?" Sloane pushed. "Something happened just now. This is important, Avery. What did I say? What garnered this reaction? Please. Stay with this."

"I get it now," Avery said. "*I'm* the problem. I've always been the problem."

"You are not the—"

She walked out.

CHAPTER THIRTY TWO

Avery had abandoned drunken bouts in the morning long ago, but after her session with Sloane, work seemed like the last place she should be. She felt fractured, broken up, and she hated what she saw.

There was always a bar, someplace, where she could get a drink, and Avery found one, a complete dive that had been open all night.

Sunlight was left behind as she walked into a dark room that stank of stale liquor. Two men were arguing in the back. The bartender was trying to solve it.

"Too early for this shit!" he yelled. "Take it home."

"I need a drink," Avery called.

"Sorry, but we're closed."

Avery flashed her badge.

"You just opened."

"*And we just opened,*" the bartender echoed. "What'll it be?"

"Whiskey, straight up. *Anything,*" she said.

"Coming right up."

Avery sat down and mulled over what had happened in Sloane's office. The tears had been about to come. If she'd stayed there any longer she would have broken down. *Why?* she wondered. She heard her father's shotgun, and kids shouting and pummeling her with fists.

Tears filled her eyes.

You can cry in front of a psycho killer but you can't cry in front of a kind, gentle shrink. You really are fucked up.

The drink came and she downed it.

"Another," she said.

No room for anyone, she thought. *You're built this way. You learned this, early on. The only way to survive is to fight, and when you're in a fight, you can't really stop to smell the roses. You're not* always *fighting,* she tried to tell herself. *You're grown up now. You're not that young girl anymore. The problem is: you're using the same coping mechanisms.* Avery laughed. A former therapist had told her that once.

She opened the killer's letter.

So you know me? she thought. *Well, bring it on. I don't know if you heard, but catching killers is all I do, all the time.*

What do we know? she asked. *Victim number one is a Gemini and she was killed like that sign. What about victim number two? Arg*, she mentally cried. *Why doesn't that add up?*

"Where's my other drink?" she shouted.

"Coming right up, miss!"

On her phone, Avery typed in Aquarius and looked in the images section. She scrolled through. Everyone had jugs of water or were splashed in water. *Catherine Williams was a Virgo. Virgo. She had no flowers in her hair.*

Avery ran the same search for Virgo. The same images came up with women and flowers, but there were a lot of others. Many of the women held balancing scales. She continued to scroll down on her phone. Suddenly, wheat was everywhere: women holding wheat; women standing on wheat and holding scales, women surrounded by wheat.

It was right in front of me, she realized. *I just didn't search long enough. Williams was a Virgo. Wheat. That's what she was holding in her hand.*

What are you trying to tell us? she wondered. *You killed a Gemini? You killed a Virgo? What do they have in common?*

She typed the question into her phone. All she received were answers about how the two signs could make a compatible relationship.

You went to Boston University. You either worked at Venemeer's bookstore or the occult bookstore. Thompson is compiling a list of people at Boston University that attended Williams' class and both shops.

What else? What else?

CHAPTER THIRTY THREE

Avery had never been to an astrologer, but she guessed one of her friends had.

She made a quick call to forensics specialist Randy Johnson.

"Hey," Randy answered. "What's up?"

"It was the wheat," Avery said.

"Not really clear on what you mean," Randy replied.

"The victim in the water was an astronomy professor, and she was made to hold wheat. That's what fell out of her hand. The killer is motivated by astrology. First victim was made to look like the sign of Gemini, second victim was Virgo."

"Whoa," Randy said.

"I need some advice. Have you ever been to an astrologer?"

"*Of course!*" Randy howled. "And a few psychics and mediums, too. Those people are *real*. I don't care what everyone else says."

"Any astrologers you trust? I need an expert to help me understand what I'm seeing."

"You *must* see Davi," Randy said.

"Davi?"

"I don't know the rest of his name. He just goes by Davi. Fantastic. Knows everything. Tell him I referred you. You can get a discount!"

"I'm not going for myself."

"You should. I heard about Ramirez. Ouch."

"*Nothing* happened."

"That's not what *I* heard."

"Just give me the number and address."

*

Davi never picked up the phone, so Avery drove to his location. The Boylston Street apartment was in a large building that could have been an office or residence. She parked and tried his number again. The voice on the answering machine harked to a big, strong, and bright strong personality.

Avery left a message.

"This is Detective Black of the A1 Homicide Division. I need to speak with you about a case. Please call me back at this number."

A sleek doorman guarded the building entrance.

"Can I help you?" he asked.

Avery flashed her badge.

"Detective Black," she said. "Homicide Division. Is there a Davi here?"

The man instantly brightened at Davi's name.

"Yeah, I think he's in," he said. "He wouldn't want to be disturbed right now. A little early for him. He usually doesn't wake up until about noon."

"Get him up," she said. "This is important."

With raised brows, the doorman lifted his phone and made the call.

"He's not answering."

"I'll go up myself. What's his apartment number?"

"Ma'am, you can't—"

"*Detective*," she said. "*Detective* Avery Black. Homicide Division. I'm on a homicide case. Two women have already been murdered. I need his help. Are you really going to stand in the way of an ongoing investigation?"

"Hold on one second," he said. "Jimmy," he called to a porter. "Can you take her up to Six B? Davi's place? Knock on the door. If he doesn't answer bring her back down, OK? And if he does answer, give him my apologies. I don't want any bad karma."

Jimmy was a slight Columbian man in a gray service suit. He put down his broom and headed to the elevator without a glance at Avery.

They headed up together.

At 6B, Jimmy knocked and listened. He knocked again and shrugged.

"He not there," he said.

"He's there. *Open up!*" Avery shouted. "*It's the police.*"

A faint voice came from inside.

"Hold on, hold on. What *is* all this racket?"

The door opened.

A robust man that Avery guessed might have been Saudi Arabian appeared in the threshold. He was dressed in a white gown. A sleeping mask was pushed up over his short black hair. He had chubby cheeks, small, expressive eyes, and a goatee, and whenever he spoke, a whirlwind of hand gestures accompanied his effeminate tone.

"Jimmy, what the hell is going on?" he demanded. "I was in dreamland just now. Who's on duty? Was that Tommy? He *knows* that dreamland is my special place. How am I supposed to have back-to-back appointments when I can't even keep my eyes open?"

"Mr. Tommy apologize," Jimmy said with a slight bow and walked away.

"Who are *you*?" Davi pointed.

Avery opened her badge.

"Avery Black. Homicide detective. We need to talk."

"Oh no," he said and snapped his fingers above his head. "Not with *that* energy. Settle down, girl. You can't come into *my* apartment until you suck back the *crazy* and bring out the inner gentle that I know is hidden in that mess somewhere."

"We don't have time for this," Avery groaned.

"You'll *make* time," he assured her. "Do you have a warrant? Are you arresting me for something? Oh, no. I didn't think so. Do it with me," he demanded. "Close your eyes. Take in a deep breath. Your eyes aren't closed. Should I close my door and go back to sleep? Because that's where I am right now."

Avery closed her eyes.

"Deep breath," he said.

She took a deep breath.

"That's right. Now breathe out slowly and allow all that crazy to go with it. *Whew, honey,* your breath stinks! Who drinks this early in the morning? We've got to get you a breath mint. No, no. Don't break the routine. Breathe in. Breathe out. Just breathe that way. That's it. Nice and easy. See there. How does that make you feel?"

The breathing helped. Avery lost some of her anxiety and edge, and by the time she was through, she had to admit she felt better.

"Good," she said.

"Excellent." He nodded. "Now what do you want?"

"Can I come in?"

"Sure." He waved. "Follow me. Who do I get to blame for having a crazy-energy-cop show up unannounced and disturb my beauty sleep?"

"Randy Johnson," she said.

"*Randy?* I should have known. She has a Saturn-Neptune aspect in her third house this month. Like oil and water. Lots of problems with communication. This," he said and indicated Avery, "would be a problem."

Davi's apartment, which Avery guessed also served as his office, was a small one-bedroom that was immaculately clean. Only two small bookshelves lined the walls. A dining room table by the window seemed to serve as an office; there was a computer along with numerous books on top of it, and one of the bookshelves was right beside it.

"Step into my office," he said and sat down at the table. "What can I do for you?"

"Can't *you* tell *me*?"

"I'm not a psychic, honey. I'm an astrologer. I don't read minds. I read the pattern of the celestial bodies. Yes, I do get impressions sometimes, but I try to hold off on judgments until I see your chart. You're a Taurus, right?"

"How do you know *that*?"

"Stubborn and self-indulgent. Sit down."

"I need some help with a case I'm working on," she said.

"Astrology killer?"

"That's right."

"Been reading about it in the papers," he casually replied with a limp wrist. "What do you know about astrology?"

"Not much."

"Well, here's a quickie lesson: when you're born, at a specific time and a specific place, the planets in the solar system are in a certain location, and that location forms your birth chart. Looks like a wheel with twelve slots. It shows you where all your planets were at the time, and what that means for you. For example, I was born in August. That makes me a Leo. Leo is ruled by the sun. The sun was in my fifth house, and that house has to do with creativity, so I'm very creative."

Avery looked lost.

"Let's just say," he went on, "that you were born in water. Don't you think you'd be more drawn to water as you get older?"

"Yeah," she said. "That makes sense."

"Astrology is like that. The planets are in a certain alignment at birth, and over time, similar alignments have shown researchers that similar personality traits can develop."

"But there must be millions of people that are Taurus, or Gemini. How do you account for all those differences?"

"Lots of ways," he said as he began to type on his computer. "It's not just your *sun* sign which makes you a Taurus or Gemini. It's also the position of the moon when you were born. And what planet was rising over the earth when you were born. Then, once you have all that, it's the time and place you were born, which can be very specific. All those differences create variety in the birth chart, and variety in individuals."

Avery pulled out the killer's note.

"Do these degrees have something to do with that?"

Davi looked it over.

"He's given you the three major points in everyone's birth chart: sun sign, rising sign, and where the moon was positioned, and he's given you the degrees. That's a lot of information, but watch what happens when I plug in those variables."

He turned his computer so Avery could see.

A long list appeared on the screen and continued to get longer.

"Here we have all the times in the last sixty years that the sun was in Sagittarius, the moon was in Scorpio, and the rising sign was a Libra. There's a lot, right? These numbers here indicate the date, time, and location on the planet. My guess is the killer is giving you a birthday, but you're the only one that can spot the date that has actual meaning to *you*. The letter was addressed to you, right? That means you're the key. Any of these dates look familiar?"

The list seemed endless.

"Not really," she said. "Can I get a printout of that?"

"Sure."

"The two victims," Avery said. "They were positioned to look like signs. The first was a Gemini. The second was a Virgo. Does that mean anything to you?"

Davi shrugged.

"Not many similarities there. They're both very adaptable, ruled by the same planet, Mercury, which is the messenger, both mutable."

"Mutable? What's that?"

"Mutable, Fixed, and Cardinal," he said. "You've got twelve signs, right? The signs are grouped into fours. First four signs are considered Cardinal signs, which means they bring about change. Aries, Cancer, Libra, and Capricorn. Each one of them indicates a change in the seasons. Change means new beginnings, both in the outside world and in your personal life. Then you have your Fixed signs, securely placed, which means they don't really change a lot. Taurus, Leo, Scorpio, and Aquarius. They're stable signs, firm, dependable. You've already had a big change in your life or in the seasons with the Cardinal signs, right? These next four signs keep everything at status quo for a while. Last but not least, you have your Mutable signs. These indicate big change, adaptability. They break things down. Think the phoenix that rises from the ash. Mutable signs destroy the phoenix while Cardinal signs bring it back. Mutable signs are Gemini, Virgo, Sagittarius, and Pisces."

Gemini and Virgo are both mutable, Avery thought. *Sagittarius is mutable. What do they have in common? The letter indicates Sagittarius.*

"I have a book here," Davi said and handed over a large, oversized paperback. "Maybe it can help. It's all about astrology, and specifically about astrology *this year*. There's a general section and a personal section. So you turn to the page on your personal astrology and it will tell you what you'll be dealing with this year, both good and bad. Turn to the page on general and it will give a general overview of our planetary astrology during the year."

Avery picked up the giant tome.

"Thanks," she said.

Davi checked his watch.

"That book," he said, "plus the printout, should help you. But if you need anything else, don't hesitate to call. You've got to go now because I have an appointment in ten minutes. That will be two hundred dollars."

"What?"

"*What?* You think these services come for free?" he said. "You interrupt my sleep, come into my house, get a free astrology seminar, a book and a printout that can help you decode your serial killer letter, and you're complaining about two hundred bucks?"

"I'm trying to catch a killer."

"Everyone's trying to do *something*, honey. I take cash or credit."

Avery paid with a credit card and headed out.

The book was under her arm, but the printout was in her hand. There were six pages with a lot of numbers in tiny font. They were birthdays that started in the early fifties. She moved down the list and tried to find one that mattered.

Nineteen fifties.

Nineteen sixties.

Nineteen seventies.

Nineteen eighties.

By the time she reached the 1990s, she was out of the building and on the street.

Nineteen ninety-seven...

Nineteen ninety-eight...

A cold chill made her stop, and for a second, she was unable to move or think.

A birthday was listed. It was one among hundreds—tiny, hard to read, and stuck between so many dates—but Avery was familiar with it. Very familiar.

It was Rose's birthday.

Rose, she thought with dread and turned around to view the people and buildings around her as if the killer could have been anywhere. That was what his letter meant.

It was a warning.

He's going after Rose.

CHAPTER THIRTY FOUR

Avery hit the police lights and tore through the city.

"Rose?" she called into her phone. "Honey, listen to me. I need you to call me back as soon as you get this call. Do you understand? I know you hate me right now, but this is very important. Please. Rose?"

She dialed again and again.

Every time, the phone went to voicemail.

Her daughter lived somewhere on the Northeastern campus. *Where?* Avery thought and wracked her brain. The name was right there in her head. They'd been unloading boxes. Rose had mentioned the house and was excited because it seemed to be slightly off-campus on a residential street. *Hemhaw? Heehaw? That's what she'd called it but that's not the actual name.* Suddenly, it came to her and she slowed down and loaded the GPS.

Backup, she thought. *You need backup.*

Her first instinct was to call Ramirez.

First relax, she told herself. *It's the middle of the day. No one is going to abduct your daughter in the middle of the day. What if she was abducted last night?* she worried.

She dialed Rose again.

"Rose, please, you've got to pick up!"

The dean, she thought. *You're going to need keys into the building. How could the killer get into a college dorm building? That doesn't matter right now! Don't cause a panic. Not yet. Nothing has happened. Get there and assess the situation.*

Rose's dorm was an average four-story building on one of the campus's main strips. The bottom half was a white-gray stone; from the second floor up it was red.

Avery parked on the street, her car askew and lights flashing.

No doorman worked the building. The glass doors were locked and there were cameras outside and in the foyer.

Calm down, she reminded herself. *No one could have gotten in here. Too much traffic.*

Sure enough, a second later a young girl opened the door.

Avery immediately flashed her badge.

"Rose," she said. "Rose Black. What room is she in?"

"What?"

"*Rose Black.* She's a freshman here. She's about this high. Blond hair. Blue eyes. Looks a lot like me? Loves to cop an attitude?"

"I'm sorry but I don't know her."

Avery moved inside the building.

The lobby opened up into two long hallways. An elevator bank was directly ahead.

Where are you? Where are you?

She tried the phone again.

Voicemail.

Avery hung up and thought about calling Jack. *You call Jack and he's just going to panic and come down here and you'll have to hear about how you're the worst mother all over again.*

Two more students appeared.

"Detective Black. Boston A1," she said and flashed her badge. "I'm looking for Rose Black. A freshman that lives in this dorm. Do you know her?"

One of the boys nodded.

"Yeah. I know her. She lives on my floor."

"*A room,*" Avery snapped. "Please. I need a room right now."

The boy turned to his friend.

"What is it, Tovi? Four E? Four D? I always forget."

"I think it's Four E," his friend said, "because she's right next to Lydia."

"Yeah, that's it." He nodded. "Four E."

Avery raced up the stairs.

Don't let my daughter be dead, she prayed. *Don't think those thoughts!* she yelled at herself. *Let her be safe,* she corrected. *Please. I'll be a better mother. I'll call more. I promise,* she swore to whoever might be listening. *I swear.*

At the fourth floor, Avery kept her eyes on the door numbers.

The hall was tan-colored with brown carpeting.

She placed her back to the wall, right beside Rose's door, and unholstered her gun. With her left hand, she knocked.

"Rose?" she called out. "Are you in there?"

The door was unlocked.

Shit, Avery thought.

A quick glance at the door's edge revealed it was broken. *No,* she thought on closer inspection. *Not broken.* It was like someone had glued both the inner locking mechanisms so they wouldn't shut properly.

She peeked her head inside the room.

Empty.

A roll along the threshold took her inside.

The room was very spacious, with two couches, a TV, and kitchen area. *She shares it with two other roommates,* Avery remembered. To the right was a small hall that led to two of the bedrooms. To the left, she could see a single bedroom.

Avery kept her gun pointed up, and at every new angle or room, she aimed on the slim chance that the killer was still there. She checked the two bedrooms first. Both were empty. Back in the living room, she inched her way across the carpeted floor to the lone bedroom. The door was closed.

She put her hand on the knob, turned, and jumped inside.

Rose was in a towel with headphones on. A small iPod was attached to the towel, and she was singing along with the tune in her ears and dancing. A spin and she noticed Avery and the gun and she screamed.

"*Ahh!*"

"Oh my god, honey," Avery said.

She grabbed Rose around the neck and kissed her forehead.

"Thank god you're all right."

Rose pushed her away.

"*Mom!* What the hell? What are you doing here?"

Avery ignored her to check the closet in her room, and under the bed.

"You're alone, right?" she said. "Has anyone come by here recently? Either last night or this morning? Anyone that seemed out of the ordinary? A mechanic? Electrician?"

"Mom, what the *hell* is going on? You're freaking me out."

"Answer me. Please, Rose. Just answer the question."

"No. No one has come by. Why?"

"The door is broke," Avery said. "Why is the door broke?"

Rose rolled her eyes.

"I don't know," she said. "Probably some stupid college prank. It was like that yesterday afternoon. The floor RA said he was going to fix it by tonight. It's no big deal. There are cameras everywhere. No one is going to come in and steal anything. *What* are you doing here?" she asked again. "Answer me!"

Avery pulled out a copy of the killer's latest note.

"That killer," Avery said and handed it to Rose. "The one that made me miss our picnic? He sent another letter to the paper. It was addressed to me. I must be getting close. He doesn't like it. He made a threat. With some help, I was able to decipher it today. Your birthdate is on that list. He threatened you, Rose. Now your door is broken—"

Rose turned red with anger.

"This is pathetic, you know that, right? *Pathetic*. Is this the only way you can think of to get back into my life? You create some fantastic scenario and scare me half to death?"

"Rose."

"*You're out of your mind.* You're *totally* out of your mind."

Rose tried to push her away.

"I'm not going anywhere," Avery said.

"I want to get dressed. Get out of my room."

"You're not leaving my sight."

She holstered her gun and called it in on her walkie-talkie.

"I need backup. Right now," and she gave the address. "I have reason to believe our killer has targeted my daughter. Get here as fast as you can."

CHAPTER THIRTY FIVE

Dylan Connelly showed up with Thompson. They were with two other officers Avery had seen around but had never officially met.

Rose was dressed and seething on the living room couch.

"I'm being held prisoner!" she yelled at the police as they walked in the door. "Can you get this crazy psycho mother out of my room!?"

Connelly had a concerned look on his face.

"What happened?"

"I broke the killer's code on the second letter," Avery said. "He gave us a list of dates, dates that wouldn't mean anything to anyone else. Rose's birthday was on it."

"How many dates are we talking about?"

"Hundreds."

"Hundreds?" Connelly noted. "What if it's just a coincidence?"

"It's not a coincidence. He wanted me to find it. He's targeting Rose. She's a mutable sign. He's already killed two other mutable signs."

Connelly waved his hands around his head.

"Whoa, whoa," he said. "Slow down. What the hell are you talking about?"

Thompson was so big he could barely fit through the door. At the mention of mutable signs, he nodded in understanding.

"Mutable signs break things down," he said. "They're like the fire that burns a building, but in a good way because the building gets to be rebuilt."

Connelly glanced over at him.

"Did I ask you?"

"I thought it was a general question."

"Mutable," Avery said. "It's a type of sign. Gemini, Virgo, Sagittarius, and Pisces. They're all mutable signs, adaptable, changing. The killer has already killed a Gemini and a Virgo. Rose is a Sagittarius. She's on that list. I'm telling you, she's been targeted. The door is broke. Look at the door!"

Connelly ran his hands along the door frame.

"Could have been a college prank."

"That's what *I* said," Rose yelled.

"It's *not* a college prank," Avery snapped. "*I'm not crazy.* That's exactly what the killer wants you to think. He did this to send me a message."

"All right, all right," Connelly moaned, "let's take this one step at a time. Thompson, check all the cameras. Make sure they're working properly. Sullivan, see if you can't track down the supervisor of this hall. We want access to the camera room. Fagen," he said to the last officer, "knock on every door in this hall. Ask if any of the students have noticed anything suspicious in the last—" And he glanced at Avery for the rest.

"Two days," she said. "The lock was broken yesterday. He would have been here. Someone dressed as a mechanic or electrician or school official. Basically, someone that looked official in some way and was tampering with that lock. Where are your roommates?" she asked Rose.

"They're at class."

"Somebody must have let this guy in. Maybe it was one of them. Do you know what classes they're in? Where they are?"

Rose gave her the information.

"Fagen," Connelly said. "Forget about knocking on doors. I'll handle that. Just go after the two roommates. We'll need to take statements. Are you all right?" he said to Avery. "You look pretty shaken up."

"Since when do you care?" Avery snapped.

Harsh, she thought the second the words had left her mouth. *You have to calm down. Relax. Breathe in like you did at Davi's.* Although Connelly had been a real jerk on her first homicide case, he'd eventually come around. Since then, they rarely had much contact, despite the fact that he was technically her supervisor.

"Sorry," Avery quickly recovered. "I think I'm just in shock. How could someone get so deep into a college dorm?"

"That's what we're here to figure out," Connelly said. "For right now, just try and relax. Take a seat. Let me and the boys handle things for a while."

"Can I please leave?" Rose demanded with her arms folded.

"Listen," Connelly said. "Even if your mother is wrong on this one, she's all stressed out right now because she cares about you. Try to remember that. And what happens if she's right? Good to have a mom like this on your side."

Connelly seemed genuinely empathetic in that moment, fatherly, and it made Avery look at him in a completely different light.

"Why are you being so nice to me?" she asked.

"What do you mean?"

"You're never nice."

He made a face at her and flicked his wrist.

137

"Come *on*," he howled. "You're a fuck-up and you know it. Half the time, you do whatever you want. You don't care about protocol or anyone else. Sure, you're smart. You solve cases. You're a good cop, but you rub everyone the wrong way, including me. It's fucking annoying. You're like a little bug that keeps buzzing in my ear. But we're supposed to be a team, right?" He looked her in the eyes. "And teams stick together."

Thompson appeared panicked when he came back into the room.

"The cameras are fucked," he said.

"What do you mean 'the cameras are fucked'?" Connelly demanded. "Don't just come in here and say shit like that. Can't you see we've got a young girl here?"

Rose was listening from the couch.

"Sorry," Thompson said and lowered his voice. "There are two cameras on every floor, one on each side. On *this* floor, the one at the other end is fine, but the closer one has some kind of filmy substance on it. Looks fine from a casual glance, but if you slide your finger over it you can feel the stuff, like a glaze. Elevator camera has the same residue, and so do the cameras in the lobby."

"Shit," Connelly whispered.

"I *knew* it," Avery said. "I *knew* he'd been here."

Rose rubbed herself from a chill. She'd heard most of it, and the realization that it hadn't been a prank, that maybe someone had purposefully destroyed her lock, was hard to absorb. She glanced at Avery and found her mother staring right back at her.

"We'll get him," Avery said. "It's going to be fine. You're all right."

"What do we do now?" Thompson wondered.

"How far did you get on the BU list for Professor Williams?" Avery asked.

"They're going to send me a complete list by the end of the day."

"What about the bookstores?"

"I already have that," Thompson said. "The spiritual bookstore gave me twelve names. The other one had a lot more: twenty-two. Out of all of them, about half were women."

"So we've got at least sixteen or seventeen names with a possible killer on them. He definitely came here. *Somebody* had to have seen him. If we can get a sketch that will narrow down the search."

She turned to Connelly.

"How many safe houses do we have open?"

"Right now? Probably two."

"Can we get Rose into one?"

"Of course," he said. "I can arrange that."

"A safe house?" Rose worried.

"No way are you staying here," Avery swore. "No *way*."

CHAPTER THIRTY SIX

The safe house was located in the wealthy section of Beacon Hill. Avery drove Rose while Connelly led the way. Rose complained the entire time.

"I can't believe this is happening."

"It's for your own protection," Avery insisted.

"Because of *you*," Rose spit. "*You're* the reason this is happening. Why don't you just stay out of my life? You always make things worse."

Anger welled up inside of Avery.

"I've had just about enough of this," she snapped. "You're my daughter. I care about you, I pay for your college, and I'm trying to save your life."

"I don't need your money!" Rose fired back. "I can get a scholarship. I don't need *you* at all! When were you ever there for me? Huh? *When!?*"

"*Right now!*" Avery screamed. "I'm here right now!"

She lowered her voice and continued.

"I know I was a shitty mom. I'm tired of hearing about it. I know I let you down a hundred times, and I let you down again this week. I'm sorry. How many times do I have to say I'm sorry?" Avery cried, then yelled, "*Because I'm getting really sick of it!* This is who I am. I'm trying to be better, I swear I am, *but this is who I am!* Either try to accept me, or go right ahead: cut all ties. This can be the last time you see me again. But you *are* going to that safe house, and you *will* stay there until I catch this guy. And if you're not happy with that I can always arrest you and put you in a jail cell at the A1."

Silence followed.

Avery kept glancing at her rearview mirror to make sure they weren't being followed. The killer had gotten under her skin; he'd invaded her life, taken a bold move against her daughter, and Avery had no idea how. In her mind, his persona had grown a thousandfold.

"What am I going to do at an empty house?" Rose complained. "You won't even give me a computer or a phone."

"You've got your books," Avery said. "I'll have someone bring you your assignments. Computers and phones can be tracked. You need to disappear. It's the only way I'll feel confident that you're safe."

Rose glanced out the window.

"I wish I had a *real* mom," she whispered.

The words cut deep. Tears formed in Avery's eyes; she bit her lip and pushed them back. Images of her own mother were hard to face: the woman was usually drunk, rarely around, and extremely abusive. *Are you like her?* Avery wondered. *No,* she firmly declared. *You're nothing like her. You might not be the* best *mom, but you're here, and you try.*

"Accept me as I am or stop speaking to me after this," Avery whispered. "Those are your only two choices. Because I *am* a real mom."

Ahead of them, Connelly slowed down on a shady, tree-lined street beside a series of brownstones. One of them, less well kept than the others, had stairs leading down and a camera overhead to check visitors. Connelly parked, got out, and scanned the area. He took the keys from his belt and waved Avery on.

"This is it," Avery said. "Follow me and keep your head low."

Connelly used two keys on three locks.

They moved inside the first floor of the large, empty apartment. Thick crimson curtains blocked out the light. Floors were wooden and bare. In the living room, there was a couch and a television set. The kitchen had a microwave and a stove. A number of frozen dinners and soft drinks were in the refrigerator. There were two bedrooms toward the back. Both of them held beds with dressers and nothing more. Clean sheets and pillows were in a linen closet. A small backyard had overgrown grass.

Connelly checked everywhere: rooms, closets, both bathrooms, the locks on the windows, and the backyard before he returned.

"You should be all right here," he said. "If you don't mind being alone for a few hours, I can send someone over tonight to keep you company. The house is fully stocked. There are cameras everywhere except the bathroom, so that's where you should go for some privacy. Back and front doors are both double-locked. We also have hidden cameras across the street in some trees that face the building, as well as in the back. No one can get to you here. I promise."

"Great," Rose mumbled. "Thanks."

"Here are the keys," he said to Avery. "I'm going to get back to the college dorm and see if anything has developed. When you're ready, you can relieve me and my men."

"Thanks," Avery said. "For all of this."

Connelly gave a sheepish nod and headed out.

Alone, the two of them appeared like strangers. Rose had her back turned in the kitchen. She ran a finger over the counter and groaned at the dust. Avery sighed and glanced around.

"You've got a TV and food. You need anything else?"

Rose shook her head.

"OK then," Avery said. "I'm heading back to the university."

She turned to leave.

"*Wait*," Rose said.

Back turned to Avery, she mumbled, "I'm sorry. What I said in the car. That wasn't right. I'm still angry, it just, wasn't right."

Avery hugged her from behind.

"I love you," she whispered. "I'm sorry I always seem to let you down."

CHAPTER THIRTY SEVEN

Avery was surprised that so much had happened in the short time she'd been away. Rose's dorm room was filled with Rose's two roommates, Thompson, Fagen, Connelly, and a sketch artist Avery had never seen before. A locksmith was already at work on the door.

"Fill me in," Avery whispered to Connelly.

"Fagen pulled both of the girls from their classes. Turns out they were here when the guy showed up. He came yesterday afternoon: tall, maybe around six-two, and was dressed like a service agent in a green jumpsuit. Maybe Spanish or Latino, they couldn't be sure. Very light skinned, green eyes, older. Walked with a limp. Thompson knew a sketch guy that could come in immediately. The dean and campus security have been alerted. The lock is being fixed," he noted, "and a guard will be posted on the street for the next few days. Nobody wants this to be made public. I assigned Sullivan to watch the safe house."

"That's him," one of the girls pointed. "That's the guy."

The sketch artist looked up; he was a thin, balding man with a short gray beard. On his lap was a large piece of white drawing paper. The image depicted was of an older Hispanic man with a shaved head and big, light eyes. He had a medium-sized forehead, high cheekbones, a strong chin, and small lips and nose. His neck was thick. The sketch ended around his shoulders.

"Yeah, that's definitely him." The other girl nodded. "He creeped me out. I mean, he was so nice and smiled a lot, but his eyes. It was like he could see through me."

Avery took the picture.

"Let's post this," she said to Thompson. "Let's not give him anywhere to hide. Make copies. Give it to the media. I want him on every news channel and in every paper by tonight."

"On it."

"*And I want those bookstore lists,*" Avery called after him.

"Are we good here?" Connelly asked. "I've got to move."

"Yeah," she said. "Thanks again."

"No problem."

Connelly left with the sketch artist and Fagen.

"You two going to be all right?" Avery asked the girls.

"Yeah, I guess," one of them said. "This is really crazy."

"The lock is being fixed," Avery said, "and you'll have a security guard watching the building until we resolve this. There's

143

nothing to worry about. Neither one of you were targets. This guy was just looking to scare me through Rose."

"Where is she?"

"Safe," Avery said, "out of harm's way."

She handed both of them a card.

"If anything happens, if you get scared or just want to talk, please call me. Rose should be back in a few days."

*

Dirty and sweaty and exhausted from the constant rush of adrenaline all afternoon, Avery drove home to take a shower and change before she headed back to the office.

In the shower, water washed away the grime, but Avery was still mentally charged.

We've got a sketch, she thought. *A name is on the way. Once those names connect, we'll have him. The Northeastern girls are safe. What's left? Go into the office,* she told herself. *Make sure Thompson has posted those pictures and plugged that face into the system. Check those bookstore lists yourself. Check on Rose. Bring her dinner.*

A quick clothing change and Avery felt like new.

The sun had already set by the time she headed outside.

Street lamps lit the area.

She'd parked quickly and on the curb instead of the designated spot she'd been assigned. Her black, fully jacked police vehicle that doubled as an average, ordinary sports car was exactly where she'd left it with one noticeable difference: a letter had been left on the windshield.

The calm, more assured air she felt after the shower and clothing swap immediately dissipated, and Avery became fully aware of her neighborhood. Every house was scanned, the side streets and dark corners.

A man about a half block away had his back turned. He was bald and slightly shaded like a light-skinned Hispanic. He wore a heavy jacket despite the warm weather, jeans, and thick shoes. There was a hop in his step, and Avery couldn't tell if it was a conscious addition, like a gangster-shuffle, or an actual limp.

She grabbed the letter.

The note was written in the same scrawled writing as the astrology killer.

I am always watching. You can't hide.

In the darkness I can see you, even when you're hiding.
I am everywhere.
Death.

Even when you're hiding, Avery read.
Does he know where Rose is hidden? Is he going after her?
The man turned around a corner.
"Hey!" Avery yelled. "*Hey!*"

CHAPTER THIRTY EIGHT

In a full sprint, Avery ran.

Her gun was out with the safety off.

"*Stop!*" she cried. "*Police!*"

The man was waiting for her when she turned the corner. His jacket was open and he pulled a gun with a long silencer on the end. The weapon made a soft, almost harmless *ptew* sound as it fired.

The night was quiet. There was a gentle breeze. Like a dream, Avery heard the gun eject bullets, and she felt the force of their trajectory as they glided past her face and arms.

She spun behind a car.

A single *pang* came from a bullet against metal and the silence returned. In the distance, there was the faint sound of an ambulance. A car beeped incessantly at some traffic jam many blocks away.

Avery shuffled toward the front of the car.

The gunman had performed the same move. Out in the open, he'd edged closer and arched around so that he had a clear shot; they were only thirty yards apart.

Avery stood up.

Both of them fired.

Avery hit him in his shooting arm. His hand dropped low but he continued to pull the trigger. Multiple bullets whizzed past her face. When his gun was empty, he twirled with a Capoeira-like move that evaded her return fire.

Despite the short distance between them and her excellent marksmanship, Avery missed every shot until her ammunition was gone.

She reached for another clip.

The attacker rushed forward.

She threw her gun in his face and kicked him in the groin. She could tell right away he was an experienced fighter. Her first blow was defended, and then his boot kicked into her stomach and she was hurled off her feet.

A passing car wailed on the horn.

The attacker jumped backward. Avery rolled out of the way. Without any thought to the scuffle in the street, the driver hit the gas and continued on.

The attacker lurched forward and stomped at Avery's head. She rolled. He kicked into her side. Avery continued to roll. The next time he threw a kick, Avery avoided it and swept his legs. The man sank to the pavement. Avery was on him.

In jujitsu school, ground-fighting had always been her passion. The idea that special moves could be performed on the ground to disable an opponent had been like another world to Avery, and she'd soaked it up.

She punched down at her attacker's throat. Again he proved that he was a seasoned fighter. Arms by his face, he evaded any serious damage, and when Avery took a breath, he struck. The man jabbed her in the stomach, pretended to twist one way and then quickly used all of his body weight to get out from under her.

Up on his feet, he ran.

Avery jumped up and gave chase.

A few people that had heard Avery's gunfire or had inadvertently stumbled on the fray appeared in doorways to point and stare.

Light rain began to fall.

The damp atmosphere blended with Avery's sweat and trickled down her face.

She was a good runner. Running had been her primary workout for years. Although she hadn't sprinted in ages, it came back to her quickly. Her legs remembered the motion. Breathing became more fluid, and her arms pumped to a rhythm all their own.

The man obviously wasn't prepared for a long struggle. A fast stumble made him sink to the street. His breathing was heavy as he darted through a breezeway. Avery kept her breathing steady and caught up to him fast.

She was twenty yards away, then ten, then five.

When she could reach out and grab him, she took two more long strides and jumped; her full body weight sank on him and they both went down. Avery made sure she was on top. She clamped her legs around his waist and leaned back. Punches to his head were deflected; she pummeled his body and waited for him to open up.

The second he tried to punch upward, Avery grabbed his arms and used them to get to his head. She caught him around the neck in a chokehold, dropped to the side, and squeezed. Legs scissored around his own legs to keep him from moving. He squirmed and fought but eventually—with the air blocked off from his lungs—he passed out. Avery squeezed him for the next five seconds—just to make sure his limp form wasn't just a ruse—and then she let go.

A quick roll and she was on her feet.

Bent over, hands on her knees, she took in slow, deep breaths.

Rain continued to trickle down her forehead and neck. Once she'd recovered from the chase and fight, she sat on top of him and cuffed his hands behind his back. A quick search revealed only a metrocard.

"You have the right to remain silent," she whispered. "Anything you say *can* and *will* be used against you in a court of law."

CHAPTER THIRTY NINE

It wasn't long before the police arrived. An ambulance came next. Two EMTs hopped out. Avery flashed her badge and pointed to the shooter's arm.

"I hit him twice," she said. "Stitch him up here."

"Did the bullets go through?"

Avery shrugged.

The EMTs quickly realized the wounds were clear of metal. The shooter was stitched and bandaged. Two officers from the D14 precinct threw him into a car and agreed to take him back to the A1. Avery followed from behind. Although she was calmer, her heart was still beating fast. *Skin tone: check. Shoe size: check. Redwings: check. Letter: check. What about his height?* she wondered. *Girls said he was six-two. This guy is maybe five-eight, five-nine. And he has brown eyes, not green.* Still, Avery knew it had to be her man. *I got him,* she thought. *I got that son of a bitch.*

Thompson met her at the station.

While the two D14 officers carried him in, Avery insisted that Thompson fingerprint him on the move and then immediately run his prints. The D14 cops put the shooter in the interrogation room and cuffed him down.

Avery retrieved a bucket from the latrine closet. She filled it up and headed back.

People along the way stood up and called out. "Yo Black, what are you doing?" "You all right?" "Who is that guy?"

She wasn't entirely rational. She knew that. In her mind, the rain still intermingled with bullets and her movement. *At any time, I could have been killed,* she thought. *Any time.*

The D14 cops were gone when Avery reached the room.

Thompson stood alone by the unconscious shooter.

"Prints are loading up now," he said.

"Get me a handwriting expert," she demanded.

"I'll see what I can do."

Avery threw the water on her suspect.

With a deep intake of breath, he leaned back and coughed for air.

"Who are you?" Avery demanded.

He was groggy and uncertain about his location.

She punched him in the face.

"Who are you!?"

Half an hour later, Avery's movements were slower and more labored. She headed back into the viewing area in frustration. The attacker tracked her from the room to behind the glass. His face had been considerably worked. Bruises lined his forehead and check. One eye was black. His nose was broken. Still, he smiled: a bloody, unforgiving smile.

"The graphology expert isn't picking up," Thompson said.

"Get me those bookstore lists."

"Coming right up."

Captain O'Malley edged into the room with a young rookie Avery had never seen.

"Heard you had a rough night," O'Malley said. "Fill me in."

"You know about the college?"

"Yeah. Connelly gave me the nuts and bolts. Is Rose all right?"

"So far so good. I called her on the way here, just to make sure. Sullivan is outside the safe house. Fagen will change shifts with him at one."

"Is that our guy?"

"That's what I'm trying to figure out. I went home to change. On the way to my car, I found a note in my windshield. Written in what seems to be the same handwriting and ink as our killer. *This* guy was walking away from his scene. I called out. He opened fire."

"Were you shot?"

"No."

"What about him?"

"Hit him twice in the arm. Ambulance stitched him up on the scene."

A calm had come to Avery after the shootout and fight and interrogation. Things appeared clearer with perspective, and the more she stared at the man behind the glass, the more he started to look like Desoto. *Like a close cousin,* she thought. *Or another brother.* Similarly, the new letter had begun to sound slightly off, as if it were written by a lowly servant rather than a fervent believer of a cause.

O'Malley sensed her conflict.

"He fits the profile, right?" he said. "Approximate age and height, ten and a half shoes, Redwing. He put the letter on your car."

"Not everything fits," she replied.

"Did you grill him?"

"Yeah."

"What did he say?"

150

Avery was disgusted by her own inability to extract a single word.

"Nothing," she said. "Not a thing."

Thompson came back in.

"This guy's clean," he said.

"*Bullshit*," Avery snapped.

"He's not in the system."

"Double-check."

"Why?"

"He's *got* to be in the system," she commanded. "He knows how to fight, shoot. Someone had to sell him those guns. He has to be connected. *Check again.*"

He handed over a single piece of paper.

"Here are your lists," he gruffly replied.

In Thompson's own hand were two lists. One was titled "Occult" and the other "Spiritual." Both had a number of names written under them, but none of the names matched up. Under occult, there were six that could have been Hispanic in origin. Five more of a Hispanic origin were on the spiritual bookstore. *Five*, Avery thought. *Five completely different names that might— might—have a connection.*

She saw it all slipping away.

"Did you run these names?" she asked.

"None of them came up," Thompson said. "Not even a parking ticket."

Avery's disbelief was hard to hide.

Thompson threw up his hands.

"*I'm telling you what I saw.*"

"What about Boston University? All the people that attended Williams' class?"

"I don't have that yet."

"Why   not?"

"We've been a little busy."

She handed him the sheet.

"Run these names again. I want photos of everyone, and information on all of them: names, birthdays, everything. This guy is good," she said. "He might have an alias, or multiple aliases. Check if any of the men are war veterans."

"How am I supposed to do that?" Thompson complained.

"*You look it up!*" Avery yelled. "You go on the Internet and you type in the names and you do some *goddamn research*!"

"Whoa, whoa, whoa," O'Malley interjected. "Everybody just calm down. Listen to me," he said to Avery. "You did a good job tonight. That guy matches everything—shoe size, approximate height, he wrote the letter and left it on your car. You had a long day. You're not thinking clearly. Go home. Take a break. We'll handle it from here." He moved closer for emphasis. "Let it go," he said.

Avery shook her head.

The ground seemed like it could open up and swallow her whole. Nothing felt right. O'Malley's caring expression lacked belief. Thompson just wanted to go home. The rookie cop raised his eyes and practically whistled from boredom.

Finally, Avery gave voice to the fears that plagued her.

"I don't believe this guy attended Boston University," she said. "Do *you* believe he worked in a *bookstore*? He looks like an entry-level thug for a Hispanic mob. You should see some of his tattoos," she snapped and stared right at O'Malley. "This might be one of Desoto's men. I can't let it go."

O'Malley completely changed. His body tightened and his gaze turned dark and definitive. He pointed a finger in her chest.

"You *will* let it go," he said. "You obviously don't know what's good for you, so I'm *telling* you: Great job today. You go home. Everyone's going to be happy. But now, you're off the case. Thompson can handle the rest. Enjoy your weekend."

Impossible, she thought. *There are too many unanswered questions.*

"You can't take me off the case," she said. "It's not over yet."

"*You're off*," he yelled. "That's it. Get out."

"I can't go."

"*You get out now or I'll have you arrested!*" he roared.

In a daze, utterly befuddled by his lack of vision and support, Avery shook her head and pushed past them all.

*

On the way home, Avery saw puzzle pieces drifting around in her mind, pieces that didn't quite fit. She wanted them to fit—*needed* them to fit, for clarity and closure. *Exhausted,* she thought and rubbed her eyes. *You're exhausted. Just go to sleep. Take a nap. Do what O'Malley said: rest.* Rest wasn't an option.

She packed a bag at her apartment. She threw in the giant astrology book Davi had given her and headed out.

At the safe house, Sullivan was parked near the front in an unmarked car. She parked her own vehicle, headed over, and leaned in the window.

"I've got this," she said. "Why don't you come back in the morning. Say eight?"

"You sure?"

"I can't let my daughter spend her first night in a safe house alone."

"Not a problem."

Rose was flipping through television channels when Avery entered. She looked up, very casual. Surprised registered at the sight of her mother's disheveled state, then relief, before a guarded expression appeared and she lowered her eyes.

"What happened to you?" she said.

"Rough night," Avery replied. "You need anything?"

"No."

Avery nodded and headed to the back room. A few pillows were thrown on the unmade bed. She grabbed a blanket and settled in.

The huge astrology tome was called *Everything Astrology*. Apparently, they came out with a new version every year. The index had all twelve zodiac signs, as well as sections on important events, relationships, and specialized concepts like trines, aspects, nodes, and lots of other names Avery couldn't understand.

She flipped right to the section on important events, expecting a moment of clarity, a symbol or sign that would make all the answers appear. None came. There seemed to be countless astrological happenings throughout the year.

June, she thought. *This month.*

In the month of June there was a list of events: *Saturn squares Neptune, June 17th. Jupiter forms a positive aspect with Pluto on June 26th. Saturn retrograde, March through August. Chiron retrograde in June. Retrograde*, she thought and looked it up. *Retrograde means a planet appears to be moving backward,* she read. *Optical illusion. A planet's power grows stronger. What does that mean?* she wondered and read on: *A planet's power is augmented, so if it's a war planet, count on more war.*

She revisited the list.

New Moon, June 5th.

New Moon? Avery thought. *That's tomorrow night.*

The next line read: *Full moon—June 20th.*

An index in the back had numerous listings for the word "mutable": *mutable cross, mutable houses,* and *mutable signs.* She turned to the pages on mutable houses and learned that each of the twelve astrological signs lived in houses, and each house had its

153

own meaning and feeling, like the money house or the house of social networking.

Her mind awhirl with gunshots and smoke and astrological concepts, Avery closed the book and closed her eyes. Nothing seemed to connect. She had a killer that *possibly* worked with the first victim and *most likely* took a class with the second. She had a facial sketch, approximate height and shoe size, and there was some astrology connection. Beyond that, it was all inferences: he was strong, big, possibly a war veteran or military man from the way he easily slipped from one kill to the next, and he was good, really, really good.

What if you're wrong? she thought. *What if these killings are random, if he's just some guy from off the street with a grudge?*

You're not wrong, she fought. *Don't go down that road. It only leads to everything falling apart. Trust your instincts. Go with your gut.*

Ramirez came to mind, but she couldn't just pick up the phone and call him. *He needs space,* she reminded herself. The distance between them affected her in the small room. All alone, without a partner or a plan, she put a hand to her face and held back tears.

CHAPTER FORTY

Avery woke up early to have breakfast with Rose. The time together was strained. Rose ate quietly, and when she was done, Rose took her coffee and prepared to head to her room.

"Is this how it's going to be from now on?" Avery asked.

"What do you mean?"

"This," Avery said. "You ignoring me."

Rose furrowed her brow.

"I've been trying to figure something out all night," she said. "Our relationship. I know you wanted to help me yesterday. That's why you came to my dorm and put me in this house. I have one question though: How is that different from anyone else? You've blown me off countless times for *other* people. Now you're helping me. So, did you do this because I'm your daughter, or would you have done it for anyone?"

"I did this for you," Avery said. "You're my daughter. *I love you.*"

A blank stare was all Rose could offer.

"Did you call Dad? Does he know I'm here?"

Shit, Avery thought.

"I was going to call him. Last night was crazy."

Rose pulled in her lips.

"I want to believe you, Mom. I want to believe you love me and that you're trying to help me and you want to make this right. It's just hard. Your actions don't always line up with what you say. How can we have a relationship if I never feel there's solid ground beneath my feet?"

Avery almost laughed.

Join the club, she thought.

Rose turned to head out of the room.

"Dad and I are close," she added. "We talk all the time. Please call him. He'll be worried if I'm not around."

"I'll call him today," she swore.

Rose stared at her for a moment, as if trying to see if Avery was telling the truth, before she headed back to her room.

In her car, Avery dialed Jack.

He picked up on the third ring.

"Avery," he sighed. "What's up?"

"I need you to stay calm and listen. Rose is in a safe house. The killer sent the station another letter. Rose's birthday was on it. We

155

went to her dorm room and there was evidence that he'd been there. She's fine now."

His reply was stern.

"Where is she?"

"I can't give you a location over the phone."

"The killer was after *you*, right? That's why he targeted Rose?"

Shame spread on Avery's face.

"That's right."

"I want to see her."

"How about tonight? We'll go to the house together."

"I want to see her now. At lunch by the latest," he demanded.

"I'm already out," she replied. "It will have to be tonight."

He cursed under his breath.

"Are you going to make me call your boss?"

Avery bristled at the threat.

"Rose wanted me to let you know she was all right. I've done that. You want to know anything else? Wait for my call."

She hung up.

Angry. She was angry and tense and uneasy on the drive. *My daughter hates me. My ex-husband hates me. My partner hates me. My boss just threw me off my case.*

The distance she felt between herself and everyone in her life was a massive expanse.

Howard, she realized.

Only Howard Randall understood. *He accepts me for who I am. He believes in me. A murderer. A psychotic killer. A prisoner.* Her thoughts turned to the psychiatrist. *Is there room in your life? For friends? Family? A lover?*

I hope so, Avery prayed. *I hope so.*

156

CHAPTER FORTY ONE

Avery had to wait a lot longer than usual at the South Bay Corrections house to see Randall.

"What's the hold-up?" she kept asking.

The woman behind the gates gave her the same pat answer.

"Someone will be with you in a minute."

Avery skimmed through a few current magazines to keep herself occupied. The activity was strangely addictive. She remembered the days when she was a lawyer, heading to the beach in her five-hundred-dollar bikinis with Rose and Jack and a bunch of tabloids in tow. *Jack hated that,* she remembered, *and so did Rose. Both of them always wanted* your *attention. You were always working so hard that any break from reality was a must.*

At that moment, she realized what Rose and Jack had been trying to tell her over the last few days. Love meant giving up certain things for the happiness of others, and Avery had been very stingy in that department. Work *was* her life, and it always had been, from the moment she had bolted out of Ohio. But now, her life was *barely* a life, and the only way to fill it was to start giving up what she knew—the bottomless pit of her job—for what she wanted—a relationship with her daughter and possibly someone else.

"Sorry to keep you waiting, Detective," said one of the guards. He let her in and closed the door behind her. "Randall is in a lot of trouble. The warden said you could see him today, out of respect for the case you're on, but afterwards, all of his visitors are cut off."

"*All* of his visitors?"

"Yeah, he's got a few."

A few? Avery knew Randall had a personal life on the outside, two children and a bunch of extended family and friends, but since he'd been in prison? The idea made her feel slightly duped, and jealous. She thought she was the only one that came to see him.

"What did he do?"

"Fuckin' guy is a wizard. Seriously. He has a whole group of followers in here. Call themselves Sons of Randall. They do whatever he wants. Earlier this week, we pulled in Carlos Desoto. You know him?"

Time stopped when Avery heard the name. She knew him, of course. He was the little brother of Juan Desoto who'd been in on the gang fight.

"No," she said.

"It doesn't matter," the guard waved. "Carlos been in and out this joint for years. The Latinos keep him safe because he's the little brother of some bigshot on the outside. Not so safe anymore. He's not here for twenty-four hours when he gets gang-murdered by Randall's followers. Randall swears he had nothing to do with it, but the warden has had enough. No more visitors for a while, and he'll probably be in solitary for life."

Randall was smug when Avery entered the small gray conference room.

"Hello, Avery." He smiled.

"What did you do?" she whispered.

"Did you hear?"

"About Desoto? Yeah."

"And how did it make you feel?"

The question startled her. In truth, it made her feel incredible and protected, but she was sickened by her own thoughts. He'd committed murder in her name.

"Why?" she asked. "*Why* did you do it?"

"The laws of the jungle are not much different from the laws of our world. Kill or be killed. An eye for an eye. You strike down one of my men, I strike down one of yours. Juan Desoto hurt you. Such a transaction cannot go unpunished."

"You killed his *brother*!"

Randall raised a brow.

"And?"

"What do you think he's going to do? Do you have any idea who he is? Juan Desoto is a legend on the outside. He's connected to everyone. He'll come after you."

Randall's old age and seemingly meek appearance flared for a moment, and Avery felt as if the spirit of a much younger man flexed and yearned to be free.

"What about *you*?" he said.

"What about me?"

"You said he'll come after *me*. Aren't you concerned about yourself?"

Avery let the question sink in.

A part of her was convinced that the man who tried kill her in the street was sent by Desoto. Maybe the letter was some kind of intimidation, or a cruel joke, she wasn't sure, but his look and attitude harked to a hired thug, not an astrological mastermind. If Desoto had sent one man, he'd send another, and another. She'd humiliated him in his own house, in front of five others, and he wouldn't stop until she'd been punished. But for some reason,

Avery wasn't worried about herself or her own possible death. All she could think about was Rose, and Jack, and Ramirez, and, strangely, Howard.

Maybe there's hope for you after all, she realized.

"No," she said, "I don't care what happens to me. I care what happens to people in my life that mean something to me."

"And *I* mean something to you?" he asked.

Avery faced him.

"Unbelievably, yes," she admitted.

Randall's eyes went glossy with tears.

"You said as much the last time you were here, and your continued appearance means more than words, but it's nice to hear, especially in this place."

"Why?" Avery asked. "I heard you have a slew of visitors."

Randall wiped his eyes.

"Do I sense a hint of jealousy?" He smiled. "It doesn't suit you, Avery."

"I need your help."

"I assumed as much."

"This killer," she said. "We have so much and yet, nothing seems to fit. I'm starting to lose perspective."

"What do you know?"

"We have a sketch, shoe size, approximate height. We believe he knew both of the victims, and from what I've seen, I think he's an astrology nut. Both bodies had eerie similarities to certain signs: Virgo and Gemini."

"Both mutable signs," he said.

"How do you know that?"

Randall dipped his head demurely.

"Astrology is a fascinating subject," he said. "One of the earliest forms of philosophy and religion. The star cycles and planetary motions have influenced countless aspects of human society throughout time. That is why people believe that if you're a Taurus, for example," he knowingly smiled at Avery, "you're considered practical, dependable, and of course extremely stubborn and independent. Wherever the constellations are when someone is born, that energy and power is said to mold and shape that person. Certain constellations bring about great loss, and vitality...and change."

"I thought maybe *change* was what he was after. Mutable signs destroy things, tear them down. Maybe he's trying to restart his life somehow, and this is the way he's doing it, by murdering people that treated him poorly."

159

"Astrologers believe that certain dates and times can be the catalyst for great change."

"I researched mutability and big events in astrology this month. I couldn't find anything that matched the pattern of these kills."

"Really?" he wondered, skeptical.

That look, Avery fumed. *He's giving me that look that means he knows something but he's not going to tell me what it is.*

"Stop playing games with me!" she demanded. "What do you know?"

A cold, distant look came to Randall.

His body seemed to shrink and tense. All the air left the room, and he was alone on his side of the table, dark and unfamiliar.

"There are certain animals that can never be tamed, Avery. They can eat out of your hand and sit on your lap for visitors, but they're wild at heart—animals. Any relationship with these creatures must be very carefully built and maintained. You have to let them be who they are, in their own environments. If you push them too hard," he said with a dangerous glare, "they just might bite."

CHAPTER FORTY TWO

Beyond the prison walls, the sun was high and bright. Avery shielded her eyes and headed to her car. The emptiness of the parking lot and the vast blue of the sky made her realize just how empty and vast her current situation had become.

The university class lists, she thought. *That's the final piece. If no names match, we're back at square one.*

Howard's question stuck in her mind.

Really? Really?

What did he mean? she wondered. *I told him I'd researched everything about the signs.*

Really?

She wanted to call Thompson and ask about the handwriting expert, and the names from the college professor's class. *You're off the case,* she reminded herself.

Relieved that the only pressure on the case came from herself, Avery hopped in her car. The astrology book was on the seat next to her.

Take everyone's advice, she thought. *Relax. What makes you happy?*

Instantly, she thought of a beach.

OK, then, she realized. *Beach day it is.*

A slow drive west took her to the M Street Beach. Avery parked the car on the boulevard and crossed the street. She found a shady spot beneath a tree. Her back to the bark, Avery settled in and opened her astrology tome.

The history of astrology began slowly, but Avery took her time. She started at page one and was determined to skim through the entire text, no matter how long it took. A large section of the first chapter was on the tides, and how the moon and other planets directly affected the tides. She glanced up at the ocean and watched the water roll onto the beach. *That's why both bodies were near the water,* she thought.

At about a quarter of the way through, Avery once again came to the section on happenings for the current year. She scrolled down the listings she had already read and flipped the page. A heading in bold stood out: *Grand Mutable Cross.* The section began: *The New Moon on June fourth activates the grand mutable cross, a powerful alignment of four planets that creates a time of tremendous change and transformation.*

Holy shit, Avery realized.

Grand mutable cross. I saw that in the index last night. June 4th. That's today.

A deeper reading revealed the planets involved: *Venus will be in Gemini, Saturn in Sagittarius, Neptune in Pisces, and Jupiter in Virgo.*

Gemini, she thought. *Virgo*.

Words and phrases stuck out: *The energy of the cross peaks at the new moon, a time to destroy the old and bring in the new, the truth will be discovered.*

A picture accompanied the text. The grand mutable cross was represented within a circular chart. The chart was drawn like a clock, with all of the planets and their respective signs around it. The "cross" itself was actually a *square* of planets. Inside the square, a cross had been drawn to indicate the name's origin, but each planet was actually on a *corner* of the square. If it had been an actual clock, the corners would have been on the numbers nine, twelve, three and six. The six and three positions held the signs Gemini and Virgo.

Avery took her phone out and mapped where the two bodies were found.

The first body had been on a yacht in the East Boston Marina. The second body was discovered in the water by Lederman Park. She took a snapshot of the image. She created a line between the two areas, and then dragged the line down to create a perfect square with ninety-degree angles. Both bottom corners were on land. *No*, she thought. *The killer would want the bodies on the ocean, near the tides*. She went back to her original line and pulled it upward into a perfect square. When the square had ninety-degree angles, every corner was by the sea. The top two points—representing Pisces and Sagittarius—were on the coast of Charlestown and in Chelsea, which was just outside of Boston.

The phone rested in Avery's lap.

This is crazy, she thought. *Grand mutable cross? That would mean there are two more bodies.*

Charlestown was in A15 territory.

Just call them, she thought. *See what comes up.*

Chelsea was just outside of Boston proper.

Chelsea police wouldn't contact us if they found a body. Maybe they found a body and thought it was an isolated incident.

The most direct route to police data from A15 was through Captain O'Malley. He'd be able to call the captain over at another division and gain any information on current homicides. *Oh well*, she realized. *Can't call O'Malley.*

162

She picked up her things and headed to the car.

The drive north on Highway 93 was quiet and solemn.

Avery kept looking to the sky, and at the empty passenger seat beside her that held the astrology book. The looming realization of a possible connection—her first in a long time—juxtaposed with the loneliness of her life. *You can't go on like this forever,* she thought. *You need a* real *life.* Drinks out with the A1 squad returned to her. It had been a good night, and she yearned for more just like that in the future.

First things first, she thought.

Chelsea was located near the Chelsea River, north of Eagle Hill, Boston. Avery took the Chelsea Street Bridge over the water and hung a left. Tanker crates and giant parking lots marked the coastline. On her phone, the exact coordinates to a possible Sagittarius kill led her to a wide area of waterfront property. She had no real expectation of what to find. The mutable grand cross idea was far-fetched, even for her, but she couldn't shake the feeling that it was exactly what the killer was up to.

Cot's Landing was a grassy, garden area complete with a children's playground, basketball courts, and a walkway to the river.

It was crawling with Chelsea police. Numerous media outlets and reporters were being corralled away to allow an ambulance to leave.

Her heart fell. Could she be right?

"Get out of this area!" a cop yelled.

"Away from the drive. *Away from the drive.*"

"The party's over!"

Avery parked and headed out.

Most of the reporters were too busy arguing with police to notice Avery. She put her black shades on and kept her head low. A quick push through a throng of people and she flashed her badge and continued on.

"Hey, that's Avery Black," she heard.

"Detective Black!?" a reporter called.

Cops turned to watch her pass. Some tried to place her face, or they gave her a hard stare as if they wondered why she'd been able to gain access.

"Yo, Black?" someone called. "What are you doing here? Aren't you a *Boston* cop?"

Avery approached the man.

"What happened here?" she asked.

"Crazy shit," he answered. "Woman was found dead, buried up to her waist in rocks and holding a bow and arrow. Can you believe that?"

Up to her waist. Bow and arrow.

The symbol for Sagittarius was a half man, half horse holding a bow and arrow.

"Do you know who she is?"

"No ID yet. She's young, maybe in her early twenties."

"Any leads?"

"Not a thing. We think the guy who did it took out all the cameras in the area. Can't figure out how. Same thing with the body. All there is are rocks and pebbles down there. Must have taken him hours to plant the body. No one saw a thing."

"Can I see it?"

"It's already out," he said and pointed to the ambulance. "We've been here all morning. Evidence is gone too, but you can head down to the water if you want."

A pathway led to a short metal banister by the river.

Avery leaned over.

Small rocks had been collected and piled near the wall as a barrier to high tides. Larger stones could be seen further out and within the water itself. A large hole in the smaller rocks was still visible from where the body had been pulled.

A worker on the rocks shouted to his partner.

"Should we close it up now?"

"Yeah, we're done here. Make it look like new."

They began to fill in the hole.

"You need something?" an officer asked.

Time had stopped for Avery. She was in her own head, in her own world, a world she solely occupied. There was sky and water and nothing else, only her and the killer. The first letter now made perfect sense. *How can you break the cycle?* He was trying to break the cycle of his own life. *The first body is set. More will come. More*, Avery thought. *More implies more than one. He needs four. He's already got three.*

He's making a real-life Grand Mutable Cross.

A second realization was obvious. *That guy that tried to gun me down wasn't the killer. He can't be. The killer was* working *last night.*

Avery checked her watch.

Three o'clock.

"Excuse me?" the officer asked again. "Can I help you?"

"Are you one of the detectives on this case?" Avery said.

164

"Yeah. Dave Brown. Who are *you*?"

"Avery Black. Homicide. A1 Division."

His eyes widened and a smile pulled on his lips.

"Oh yeah," he said. "Sure. I thought you looked familiar. What are you doing here?"

"Your murder matches the MO of a killer we've been tracking. Contact my Homicide Supervisor over at the A1, Dylan Connelly. He has information to share."

She walked off.

"Hey!" he called. "Where are you going?"

She didn't look back when she answered.

"To catch that son of a bitch."

CHAPTER FORTY THREE

O'Malley was prickly on the other end of the phone.

"What do you want?" he said.

"You've got the wrong guy in lockup," Avery replied, excited and pumped full of adrenaline. "He's probably some goon sent by Desoto."

"You told me that yesterday."

"There's another body," she added. "Up in Chelsea on the other side of the river. It was placed there last night. I'm here now. A woman was buried up to her waist. She had a bow and arrow in her hands. She matches our killer's MO. Sagittarius. The third sign. I figured it out."

"What did you figure out?"

"He's trying to create a Grand Mutable Cross, it's a rare astrological event. Four planets form a perfect square. It's supposed to usher in a new age of transformation."

"Grand mutable *what*?"

"Two of the women he killed formed half of the square. Venemeer had a shadow. She was made to look like a Gemini sign. The other one held wheat in her hand. That's a Virgo symbol. The woman here in Chelsea was made to look like a half-woman Sagittarius. She even had a bow and arrow."

"Did you see the psychologist like I told you to?"

"*Listen to me!*" she yelled. "He's got one more to go. One more kill will complete the square. Tonight is the new moon. He'll need a Pisces."

"Square? I thought you said it was a cross."

"*Dammit!*" Avery cried. "*This is real!* I want backup and a team to survey the area. I know where he's going to be next."

"You got some balls on you, Black. I'll give you that. I tell you to stay off the case, you work even harder. What the hell am I supposed to do with someone like you?"

"Give me a team."

"Even if you're right," he said, "can you prove it?"

"*Another woman is dead!*" she yelled. "Isn't that proof enough? You want to know how I found her? I just followed the corners of a square. Every kill is at a perfect ninety-degree angle from the others, *and* they're made to look like astrological signs."

O'Malley's voice went low.

"Jesus," he whispered.

166

"You don't believe me?" she said. "You want more proof? OK. At least tell me what came back from the college lists. Did we get a match?"

"You'll have to talk to your new partner—*Thompson*."

"Thompson doesn't give a shit about this case!"

O'Malley lost it.

"*Thompson's been working his ass off for you!* Do you know that? You're not the only cop that works and you're not the only cop that cares. Do you know how many cases I have to oversee right now? I've got three dead housewives on Haynes, a gang war about to break out on the Southside, drug cartels, pimps, and an illegal casino racket downtown. The only case where we have an actual suspect in custody is yours, *and you want to ignore that completely?*"

His voice turned to a cold whisper.

"The mayor thinks you did a great job. He thinks this case is solved and he's telling everyone it's all because of you. What am I supposed to do?"

"Tell him we got the wrong guy. Tell him we'll get it *right* this time."

"You really want this?" he said. "Give me something *solid*—something *real*, Avery. I don't want to just hear about dead bodies that crop up at ninety-degree angles and that one had a bow and arrow. I need a connection, a solid connection that proves you're right. You get me that and you get your team."

He hung up.

"*Shit!*" Avery yelled and slammed down the phone.

Thompson was her next call.

"What do you want?" he said, just as annoyed as O'Malley.

"Where are you?"

"I'm sitting at my desk going over the college lists like you asked me too."

Avery was genuinely surprised.

"Really?"

"Yeah, *really*. What do you think?"

"I thought you didn't believe me."

"I *don't* believe you," he snapped back. "You're probably the most stubborn, pigheaded cop on the force. You get leads and throw them away and find more leads and throw them away. You've got piles of work on your desk and you're just begging for more. It's fucking crazy. You know that, right? But you're also a freak of nature," he mumbled. "You see things, things I don't see. I'm trying to see them, too."

167

"What did you find?"

"Nothing," he said. "There have to be a thousand names here, and not one of them matches either one of the bookstore lists."

"What did the handwriting specialist say?"

"He's not here yet. Got called on a more urgent case."

"What could be more important than this?"

"You obviously haven't read the papers today. People think this case is solved. The headline is Astrology Killer in Custody. Be honest: Are you *sure* this isn't our guy? He wrote the letter. He tried to kill you."

"It can't be him," Avery said. "Another body turned up last night."

"What do you mean?"

"In Chelsea. A woman, placed by water like all the rest. Made to look like the sign of Sagittarius with a bow and arrow in her hand. The other two represent Virgo and Gemini. He's creating a square of bodies, each one at ninety-degree angles to the other. He's got three already. He needs one more. Tonight is the night."

"How do you know that?"

"It's a new moon. It's the height of this thing he's trying to create. The only thing I can't figure out is how he's doing it. How did he get into a college dorm? How did he plant these bodies without detection?"

"Maybe he's some kind of soldier," Thompson said. "Special ops, shit like that. If he's meticulous, why leave a footprint at the first scene? Why let those BU girls see his face?"

"He's toying with us," Avery said. "But I know his next move. I know exactly where he's going to be. Are you with me on this?"

Thompson hesitated.

"What did O'Malley say?"

"He said I could have a team if I found proof. I know where he's going to be next. Isn't that proof enough? He won't give the OK, but this is solid, Thompson. I'm telling you. We've got him. All we have to do is show up."

"Just the two of us?"

"No," she said. "We'll need at least two more people, and a boat. It's a large area to cover. You think we can get a boat?"

"Yeah," he said, "I can get a boat. You *sure* about this?"

Avery stared out of her open car window. The pieces were falling into place, every one of them, and only thing missing was the killer.

"I've never been more sure of anything in my life."

CHAPTER FORTY FOUR

Avery met everyone at a small, posh bar on Medford Street, just south of the Mystic River. The place was dark and busy with a young, hip crowd. She sat at a table with Thompson on her left, the small but fired-up Finley on her right, and a very somber Ramirez directly ahead. All of them wore layman's clothing and seemed out of place in the happening joint.

"Thanks for coming," Avery said to Ramirez.

"How could I say no?" He shrugged. "They stuck me with this asshole," and he pointed a thumb over at Finley.

"Aw, come on," Finley complained. "You blew it with Black. They gave you someone even better. You should be ecstatic to have me on your side."

Avery stared at Ramirez.

"I'm sorry," she said. "For everything. Truly."

"It's fine," he mumbled. "It's OK. Let's just get this over with."

Avery could tell that he wasn't fine. Sleeplessness was in his eyes, and the sharp edges of his suits and personality were dull.

He's hurting, she said. *I really hurt him.*

"Is this a lover's quarrel or a stakeout?" Finley complained.

"It's a stakeout," Avery said, and she eyed each of them in kind. "Here's what I know. Our guy is trying to create something called a Grand Mutable Cross, which is an astrology event where four planets form a perfect square. A third body was found over in Chelsea. The location of that body, along with the professor and Venemeer, form three corners of the square. The last corner is going to be somewhere around Ryan's Playground, right beside the Alford Street Bridge. Tonight is a new moon, which is supposed to be the most powerful moment of this planetary alignment, so that's where he'll be."

"We're not going to try and stop him from killing another woman?" Ramirez asked.

"How?" Avery said. "We don't know anything about him. This guy has been one step ahead of us the entire time. Our only chance is to try and catch him in the act."

"*Stakeout.*" Finley clapped with an eager smile on his face.

"This is no joke!" Thompson yelled.

"He's right," Avery said. "This guy is no joke. It's reasonable to assume he knew the first two victims, but his name doesn't match up anywhere. That means he has multiple aliases. He's also smart enough to elude cameras—and crazy enough to enter a packed university and try and abduct *my daughter* in front of hundreds of people. My guess is, he's some type of military man. Maybe a special agent or a Navy Seal. A person who can blend into environment. That means he deserves your respect, Finley."

"All right, all right," Finley said. "I got it."

"Thompson, did you get the boat?"

"Yeah," he said. "I signed it out. Said we had to check the shoreline for a body dump. But who's going to drive? I've never driven a boat before."

"I can drive," Ramirez said.

"Good." Avery nodded.

She pulled out a map.

It was a satellite image printout with square drawn on it. The edges of the square touched on all the points where the bodies were found, and the one point that was still empty.

"Here *we* are," Avery said and indicated a spot to the south of the square. "Ramirez, you'll take the boat and park it here," and she pointed to a man-made inlet about two thousand feet southeast from the stakeout point. "We don't want to scare him. No police boats in the area. We'll stay in radio contact the entire time. Finley, you'll be in an unmarked car, parked and hidden in the lot by the Alford Street Bridge. Ramirez will take the southwest. Thompson, can you shoot a long-range rifle?"

"I can shoot accurately from about three hundred yards," he said with confidence. "If it's windy, maybe less."

"Good," she said, "I'll take the diamond mound at the baseball field. You can be much further out, about two hundred yards— maybe here." She pointed. "It might be difficult to get to me if things go bad, but at that distance, he'll never guess we have someone in hiding watching our backs from afar. For added insurance, we'll both put on our worst clothes, roll around in a garbage dump for a while, and play sleeping bums. I don't want this guy to suspect a thing."

"Where do you think he'll come in?" Ramirez asked.

"If it was me?" Avery said. "I'd take the bridge and scout the area on my way over. If everything looked clear, I'd park in the lot where Finley will be placed and walk from there."

"Any cameras in the lot?"

"None that I could find anywhere in the area, but remember, this guy is a pro. He does his homework. He probably scouts every area before he goes in, possibly multiple times. He could be in the vicinity right now. All we have is a facial sketch, so be ready for anything."

"How long you think this is going to take?" Finley asked.

"Why?" Avery said. "You've got a date?"

"*It's a stakeout,*" Thompson roared.

"*I'm just wondering!*" Finley yelled.

"Prepare for an all-night affair," Avery said. "The first bodies were most likely dumped around three or four in the morning."

"When do we start?" Thompson asked.

Avery checked her watch.

Eight o'clock.

"How about eleven?" she said. "That will give everyone time to rest, eat, and get set."

Nods went all around.

"Thompson, why don't you go to the boathouse with Ramirez and make sure he gets the keys and heads out. When you're done, find a hobo outfit of some kind and meet me at my apartment. Everybody needs to wear a vest tonight, and any other armor you've got. This guy is too good to screw around. Finley, when you get to that lot, don't let anyone see you. Just act like a traveler on a long trip and you needed to stop off somewhere to take a nap. You got that? That's your motivation."

"Yeah, I got it," he said.

Ramirez appeared frustrated.

"What if he doesn't show?" he asked. "Boat costs money. We'll need to check out a sniper rifle and binoculars for everyone. That leaves a trail."

"If this goes south," Avery said, "I'll take the heat. It's all on me."

"And me," Thompson said.

"You don't have to do that," Avery offered.

"We're partners now." Thompson nodded with a stern gaze. "Right?"

Ramirez shook his head and looked away.

CHAPTER FORTY FIVE

At a thrift shop near her apartment, Avery found a pair of baggy, fly-away green pants that were way too big for her body. She bought them, along with an oversized denim shirt, a floppy gray hat, and a pair of old shoes. The outfit couldn't have been less appealing, but it was perfect. She dressed at home and even came up with a shuffle walk to accompany her old-person, drunken persona.

She rubbed some alcohol from her liquor cabinet in her palms and used it as perfume on her neck and clothes. The gun was in her holster under the denim shirt. Her ankle-knife was in place. Her phone was put on mute and the walkie-talkie on low.

At the mirror on her way out, she couldn't even recognize herself. The hat was down, her hair jutted out on both sides, and the clothing fit the part. *You look like a bag lady,* she thought. *All you need now is a cart.*

Avery had been concerned about Thompson. He was so big and distinct-looking with his light hair and skin and eyes that she worried he'd be pegged as a cop immediately. Her doubts were instantly put to rest when she saw him outside.

Thompson was dressed in dirty overalls, boots, and a dark blue shirt that was extremely large on his already big frame. The shirt practically hung down to his knees, but it was his face that sealed the deal: he wore a gray wig that made him look sixty years old, an old military helmet, and he'd done wonders with makeup. With the exception of his long-range rifle bag, she could swear he was just an old, big hobo in need of a home.

"Nice work," she said.

"You too." He nodded.

"What are you going to do with that rifle?"

He pulled out a green garbage bag.

"I'll wrap it up."

"Excellent."

"You wearing a vest?" he asked.

Avery tapped on her chest.

"Of course," she said, "You?"

Thompson smiled.

"Never leave home without it."

At ten forty-five, Avery dropped off Thompson at a large lot on Medford Street so he could walk, hitchhike, or stumble his way to his final position. The car was parked on West Street, to the west of

Thompson and the South of Finley, so that Avery, too, could go the rest of the way on foot and try to get herself into character.

She walked across the wide and heavily trafficked Alford Street and nearly got hit by multiple cars in the process. She raised her middle finger to everyone. *I think I could like this,* she thought.

Most officers hated stakeouts—waiting for hours at a time in a car or on the street, pretending to be invisible while they downed bad food and coffee. Avery had always felt the exact opposite. Stakeouts were times where she could think, and be someone different, and clear her head, not just for the case, but in her life.

Ramirez kept invading her thoughts.

She imagined him on a boat, by himself, pining over her and upset that he hadn't been given a closer assignment. *What am I supposed to do?* she wondered. *He didn't even want to be my partner. If I put him in the park with me, maybe he would have hated that too.*

Forget about him, she demanded. *What do* you *want?*

In truth, she had a strong physical connection to Ramirez, and they got along great, but the idea of a full-fledged relationship was still hard to see.

Why? she wondered. *What's wrong with him? It's not him,* she thought. *It's you.*

On the baseball diamond at Ryan Park, she worked her way toward the Harborwalk along the river's edge. A dark area lay just beneath the bridge, right before the water. *That's where I would place the next body,* she thought. *It's dark and out of the way, and once he's down there no one will be able to see him.*

Avery hopped over the fence, fell down, and lay there for a while, just in case someone was watching.

Theatre had always been something she'd loved as a child. In school plays, she could transform herself into a new person with a completely different life. For a while she even thought about being an actress. All that came to a halt when her father had discovered her passion. "You wanna be a what?" He'd laughed. "An actress? You know what those people are? *Liars,*" he'd spit. "They lie like the devil. Is that what you want? You wanna be a liar? The devil's worker? Shit, I'll kill you before that ever happens." It was the last day Avery ever thought about theatre.

Now, she knew that acting wasn't a lie. Real emotions had to be harnessed, real feelings and beliefs brought to the surface. To play a drunken hobo, she had to imagine herself in the worst place of her life—no job, no home, no prospects, nothing. It wasn't hard. After she lost her job at the law firm, she'd thought about committing suicide. Her life had taken a complete turn and she had no idea how to deal with it.

As Avery lay on the ground, waiting for any sign of the killer to appear, she realized that her father had given her one thing that she needed now more than ever: he'd taught her how to shoot, and how to hunt. Deer, jackrabbits, even birds shot from trees would be their dinner most nights. He knew how to track and skin animals, and he'd taught her most of it. The instruction had come with a never-ending list of what she couldn't do because she was a girl, but Avery had proved him wrong every time the rifle had been in her hand.

Time moved slow on stakeouts.

Instincts were heightened, but movement was nearly nonexistent. With nothing to do except blend into the surroundings and watch and wait, Avery killed time by tracking cars and staring up at the sky looking for stars. Every hour, she surreptitiously whispered into her walkie-talkie to get a bead on her team.

"Midnight," she said. "All clear."

The others answered.

"All clear."

"One o'clock. All clear."

"All clear."

At three-thirty, Finley came on the radio.

"I've got a car moving very slow over the bridge. Guy inside keeps looking around like he's checking the place out."

"Stay low," Avery whispered back.

"I'm fucking low," he complained.

Fifteen minutes later, Finley called back.

"False alarm. The guy made a U-turn and headed back over the bridge."

At four ten, Avery spotted a small, simple motorboat under the bridge.

"Wake up, wake up," she called. "Everybody stay alert and keep out of sight. There's a boat under the bridge. Ramirez, stand ready."

"Check," Ramirez called back.

"Anybody got eyes on him?" Avery called. "I'm too close. Don't want to get caught using the binoculars."

"I can see him through my long-range scope," Thompson replied. "I'm about five hundred yards east of your position, under a bench on the Harborwalk. Pretty sure he won't be able to see me. I'm looking at an athletic guy, large, dressed in a jacket and jeans. Possibly Latino. Middle-aged. He just stood up and looked around.

Now he's sitting down. Just sitting there. Seems to be waiting for something."

"Nobody move," Avery called.

The boat drifted out from under the bridge. A quick roar of the ignition and it moved right back in the shadows and became very difficult to see.

"I need eyes," Avery called.

"No change," Thompson replied. "He's just sitting there. Wait. There he goes. He's on the move. Something is in the boat. He just pulled something out. It's the size of a body."

"Everybody *stay calm*," Avery insisted. "Finley, take your car out of the lot. Drive it on the bridge and keep the west side of the bridge covered. He's in a motorboat with no hood. If he tries to run, do you think you can hit him?"

"Definitely," Finley called back.

"Good. Once you're on the bridge, Ramirez can engage. Everyone stay on alert. This guy might be armed and extremely dangerous. Don't do anything stupid."

From her position, Avery watched the man on the boat fumble with something in the dark. The object was flopped onto the side of the boat.

"I'm in position," Finley called.

"Thompson," Avery said. "You got him in your sights?"

"I've got him."

"Ramirez, you're on," she called.

Everything was silent except the cars on the bridge and the sound of the water. Avery maintained her position. She was close enough to the bridge to sprint if need be, and yet far enough away not to be noticed.

The wail of a police boat came up fast.

Avery spotted the small cruiser cutting through the river. Ramirez came into view. She watched and listened as he clicked on the loudspeaker.

"This is the police," he called. "Stay where you are."

The man dropped his load in the water and bent down out of view.

Thompson figured it out first.

"*He has a gun! He has a gun!*"

Ramirez shouted over the loudspeaker.

"Stand up so I can see you. Put your hands in the air."

The man stood up from the boat with a rifle aimed at Ramirez.

Multiple shots were fired. Glass shattered on the small police boat. Ramirez flipped out of view. The side of the boat was punctured with bullets.

Shit! Avery thought.

"Finley, don't you move," she called. "You stay right where you are."

Two muffled shots came from Avery's right: Thompson on his rifle. When she turned back to the bridge, she saw the man on the boat had been hit. With the calm of a trained soldier, he simply scanned the shoreline through his scope and opened fire again.

"*I'm hit! I'm hit,*" Thompson roared.

The shooter revved his engine and turned the boat toward the coastline.

"He's headed for the beach," Avery shouted. "Finley, get down here."

She jumped up from her position and ran along the Harborwalk.

"Thompson, where are you?" She called on the radio.

"I'm hurt," Thompson called back. "Rifle was hit. This guy is good. He shot me in the head. Helmet saved my life. I'm heading over on foot."

The police boat seemed dead in the water.

"Ramirez," Avery called. "Can you hear me? Are you hit?"

"I'm here." He waved from a prone position in his boat. "He hit the gas line or something. Boat's stalled. I'm trying to figure it out."

The shooter's craft roared out of the river and over the rocks and dirt of the shoreline. The propeller snapped with a loud crack. The man hopped out and ran up a dirt hill, holding one arm and moving with a noticeable limp. Avery had a clear shot at him.

"*Police!*" she screamed. "*Don't move!*"

Finley appeared directly in front of the man's path.

"*Police!*" he called.

The man fired from his hip.

Finley got off a few rounds; none of his shots seemed to have hit, but his own body jerked back from return fire and he sank to the ground.

"*Finley!*" Avery cried.

She fired. The man stumbled and turned to face her. A single shot from his weapon grazed Avery's thumb along with her gun and the gun flicked out of her hands.

"*Ah!*" she yelled.

Another shot tagged her in the chest and she was hurled off her feet. The vest saved her, but the pressure from the hit expelled all the air from her lungs. She sucked in air and curled into a ball.

On the ground, she searched for her team. Finley was down. Ramirez had taken to the water and was quietly swimming toward them. Thompson shuffled toward her on one good leg, but he was too far away to help.

All of us, she thought. *He took out all of us in seconds.*

With a fake groan, Avery reached for the ankle-knife. She surreptitiously cupped it in the palm of her hand and rolled to all fours. Another loud cry and she leaned back and pretended to grip her wounded chest.

The man limped toward her, his gun trained on Avery's head. As he drew near, she could see the shiny film of blood on his arms and legs. His chest, however, was clean although multiple shots were visible on his shirt and jacket.

He's wearing a vest, she realized.

He looked like the police sketch. Light-skinned and balding with gray hair, he had strange features that marked him as both a Latino and possibly German, with a strong jaw and light green eyes. She guessed he was around fifty years old by the wrinkles.

Although his movements were tough and strained from so many injuries, they also harked to a man that had been trained to stay alive at all costs. The slight movement of his head toward the water and Avery was sure he heard Ramirez. A quick look along the boardwalk and he must have spotted Thompson.

In that instant, Avery gave the performance of a lifetime.

"*Now!*" she yelled to no one behind him.

At the same moment, she sank to her right and hurled the knife.

The man, jaded from his first ambush and reluctant to be startled again, instantly fired at Avery's head and turned around to see whom she'd been calling. Since Avery was falling over, the bullet only grazed bone by the side of her left eye instead of hitting her directly in the forehead as the killer had planned.

The ruse—discovered too late—made him turn back to Avery with his gun aimed at her last position.

The knife sank into his neck.

He jerked from the shock and stumbled back. The wounds on his legs made his footing unsure and it took a second for him to ground himself and recover.

Avery swatted his gun hand away and punched him in the jaw. Not a second was wasted. She kicked a foot into his groin, and when the killer attempted to aim his gun again, she chopped his wrist. A crack resounded; his wrist went limp and the gun dropped.

The killer tackled her to the ground. Avery felt a rib crack from the force of his body slamming her into the earth. His good hand went to her neck and he tried to snuff out her life. Oddly, his eyes only emanated love and concern, and the shock of his intimate gaze momentarily stunted Avery's reaction time.

Avery squirmed beneath him to reach the knife that still dangled from his neck. Just as her hand got free, he continuously pummeled her in the head with his opposite elbow and kept his body pressed into hers. Avery saw stars. She could feel herself about to black out. With one final push, she popped her hips, cleared some room between them, and reached up.

She felt the knife in her palm.

She pulled it out to a spray of blood and stabbed him once more before the killer suddenly relented. Pressure released from Avery's body. A groan escaped his lips. His eyes fluttered shut and he slumped over.

Avery lay on the ground beside him, gasping for air.

Ramirez ran up, soaked from the water and a gun trained on their attacker.

"*Let me see your hands! Let me see your hands!*"

When he realized the man was unconscious, he checked his pulse and wounds.

"Avery, you all right?"

Avery nodded and rolled up with a painful grimace.

"I'm OK," she whispered. "How's *he*?"

"He's alive. Looks like he's losing blood fast."

"Finley." She pointed. "Check on Finley."

Thompson appeared on his radio.

"Officers down," he called. "Officer down. I've got two officers down. Suspect is down. We need an ambulance right now."

CHAPTER FORTY SIX

Two ambulances and a slew of police arrived at the same time.

Avery was able to walk slowly if she regulated her breath. She and Ramirez wordlessly remained by Finley's side; his situation seemed bleak. At one point, Avery feared he was no longer breathing. When the EMT workers appeared, they shared dreadful looks.

Thompson stood over the shooter. Medics nursed his wounds and kept the suspect alive while multiple officers from the A15 looked on.

"We need divers," Avery instructed. "He dropped a large bag in the water, right under that area of the bridge. It might be a body."

"I'll get on that," one of the officers confirmed.

"We'll escort you to the hospital," another offered.

Avery shook her head.

"I'd rather you ride along in the ambulance with our guy." Avery motioned. "He's dangerous. My partner and I will escort you from behind, just in case he tries anything."

The killer was cuffed, surrounded by police, and he lay unconscious in a pool of his own blood. Thompson raised a brow.

"He needs an escort?"

Something about the large shooter continued to keep Avery on edge.

"I loaded him with bullets and he still came after me. We had the element of surprise and he still nearly killed us all. He could be faking," she said and glanced at him, "or he could recover at any moment. We treat him as live and extremely dangerous until he's behind bars."

*

The drive to the hospital was uneventful.

In the emergency ward, the man's wrists and ankles were chained to the bed. Thompson took fingerprints and headed to the office to scan him into the system. One of the A15 officers stayed in the emergency room while the doctors worked.

Avery sat in the waiting room outside of the killer's room, her thoughts on Finley and his brave—yet stupid—lurch out from the highway to protect her.

She called Ramirez.

"Where are you?" she asked.

"Right below you. Fourth floor. Mass General."

"So close and yet so far," Avery mused.

"How's our suspect?"

"Still in surgery. Doctors say it's fifty-fifty. How about Finley?"

"Same. Doesn't look good. *You* OK?" she asked.

"Yeah," he mumbled. "How are *you*?"

"I'm still here."

A long pause followed before Ramirez gushed: "You're incredible, Avery. You know that? Despite everything that happened, you did it. You were right about this guy. Everyone thought you were crazy, but you were right. I'm amazed by you."

The praise sickened her.

She shook her head.

"I was too late," she spat. "He killed that fourth girl."

"You don't know that."

"Yeah," she said. "I know."

"You spoke to the divers?"

"No... I just know."

In the early hours of the morning, Avery went down to see Ramirez in person. He was slouched in a chair of the waiting room, eyes closed and head in his hand. At her arrival, he roused himself and offered a wane smile; Avery was still dressed in her hobo costume.

"Nice outfit," he said.

Avery smiled back, but a slew of emotions welled up inside of her at that moment. The long night, Finley in critical condition, and yet another possible dead victim made her realize she was all alone and needed support: a hug, a kiss, the gentle feeling of a man's arms around her.

Not any man's arms, she thought. *Ramirez. I want Ramirez.*

She opened up for a hug.

As always, Ramirez didn't disappoint. Up on his feet in an instant, he allowed her to melt into him.

*

At eight ten in the morning, a call from the A15 confirmed that a body had been dumped in the river, a girl with weights and a number of fish tied to her body. Avery silently mourned a victim she never knew but couldn't save.

Eventually, one of the doctors appeared.

"Your prisoner must have some past," he said. "There are healed wounds all over his body: gunshots, knife slashes, burns, you

180

name it. Looks like he's been through a war. The only time I've ever seen anything like that is with veterans. Is he a soldier?"

"We don't know," Avery replied.

"He's one tough customer. Shot six times, stabbed twice, and nearly drained of all his blood and he's still alive."

"When can I talk to him?" she asked.

"That's the crazy thing," the doctor said. "He's up now. We've been in surgery for almost three hours. He was pumped full of enough anesthesia to down an elephant, but he's awake. Just staring at the ceiling but conscious and with strong vitals."

"Did he say anything?"

"Nothing."

"Can I talk to him?"

The doctor raised his brows.

"You can try."

Avery stood up and pushed past him.

Inside the recovery room, an A15 officer was practically asleep on his feet.

"Give me a minute," Avery said.

"Thanks," he mumbled and headed out.

The man lay in his hospital bed, covered up to his torso. Multiple bullet wounds had been wrapped. Blood showed through some of them. A bandage also bound his neck. His eyes were closed but he seemed to be breathing steadily.

"Are you awake?" Avery asked.

"Yes," he whispered.

"Who are you?"

No response was given.

"Where are you from?"

"Lots of different places," he explained.

His accent was foreign.

"When did you first come to Boston?"

"Fifteen years ago," he remembered.

"Did you kill Henrietta Venemeer?"

No answer.

"Did you kill Catherine Williams…? What about that girl on the beach? What about the girl in the river? Did you kill them? Have you killed other people?"

Silence.

"Where do you live?" she asked. "What do you do?" she demanded.

The beep of his heart monitor was the only response.

Avery shook her head. He'd probably been up all night preparing for the murder. *Leave him alone,* she thought. *He's done for tonight. Get him when he's fresh.*

"You targeted my daughter," she said. "Why?"

A smile came to his face.

"She's pretty," he whispered. "Not my type, but pretty."

"Why have you done all this?" she demanded. "What was it for?"

But he wouldn't answer any more questions.

Avery grabbed the bars of his bed and leaned in close.

"You're finished," she growled. "You shot a cop. You dumped a body in the river. You'll be in prison for the rest of your life, or dead, or worse."

He smiled back, his eyes glazed over, almost as if he looked forward to it. She could see the insanity shining in his eyes and it terrified her. It penetrated her soul. It was one more look, she knew, that would make up her tapestry of nightmares.

"But I'll always be a part of you," he said. "When you close your eyes, you will see me. And that is enough for me."

He smiled wider, his eyes glazing.

As she saw that look, his expression, she suddenly knew that evil did exist. It truly did, as a separate force in the world. And that, more than anything, terrified her.

She had to look away. She knew if she stayed there one more minute she would strangle him herself.

She turned and hurried from the room, the sound of her shoes echoing in the hall. There were other monsters out there, she had to remind herself. She couldn't spend anymore time with this one.

There were one too many monsters trapped in her mind already.

CHAPTER FORTY SEVEN

The drive home was filled with regrets.

If I'd only shot to kill, Avery realized, *I could have saved Finley. If I'd figured out his name and address earlier, I could have saved that last girl.*

No matter how many times she reviewed the night—the boat coming in, the angles of the shots—it was already over. Everything had played out like it was supposed to play out, Avery realized. She just couldn't accept it.

She called Thompson.

"What do you got?" she demanded. "Who is he? Where is he from? Why did he do it?"

A long silence came, followed by a sigh.

"Perp's name is Samuel Juanez. Worked in her store, years back. No record. Not a blemish. Everyone who knew him said he was the friendliest employee they'd met. Never any problems. Not one."

Avery gasped and let it sink in. It was too much. How was it possible?

"Not one red flag?" she asked.

Silence. Then:

"Not one."

She fumed. It was unfair. Unjust. How could human nature perfectly disguise such a monster? What did that say about all the other perfectly normal people functioning all around her?

Somehow it would have been better if there had been signs. *Any* signs.

The normalcy of it all was what struck her with terror.

"Let it go," he sighed. "You did a good job. You caught him. You defied orders and put together a team and caught the son of a bitch responsible for murdering four women in our town. You were right. Take some comfort in that and move on."

How can I move on? she lamented.

The darkness and injustice of it all sickened her. They had put away a mass murderer, and without a word of explanation.

He was about to hang up.

"Thompson?" she called out.

"Yeah?"

"Thanks for tonight. You really came through. I won't forget that."

"*You* came through," Thompson pointed out. "I won't forget that, either."

Angry and without any way to absolve her anger, she imagined herself in an empty landscape of darkness and the unknown.

You're not alone, she thought, *not now, at least. Let it go...*

How? she pleaded.

She thought of a life with Ramirez, taking a ride on his boat, laughing with him at dusk and allowing herself to finally give in to love.

You can't control what happens on the job, she began to understand. *Someone else is in charge of that. But you* can *control what happens in your life. You can fix your relationship with Rose, and tell Ramirez how you really feel. Stop wasting precious time on the job and issues you can't control, and work on* your life *for a while, and the things you* can *control.*

She called Sullivan.

"You still on duty?" she asked.

"Yeah," he said, "I'm outside the safe house right now."

"You can let Rose go," Avery said. "If you don't mind, maybe just drive her back to school and see she gets into her dorm? Tell her I'll be by later to check in. Her father is probably losing his mind. Have her call him."

"I can do that," he said. "Heard you caught your guy. Who is he?"

"I wish I knew," Avery whispered and hung up. "I wish I knew."

EPILOGUE

Two weeks later, Avery was back in the hospital with a bunch of flowers for Finley. He wasn't himself. He was sitting up in bed, but his spirits were low. He greeted her without fanfare, with little more than a nod, before he turned away.

"How you doing?" she asked.

"Not good," he said.

Avery had heard it all from the doctor. His spine had been bruised; walking would be difficult, and he took a bullet to the lung. He might never be able to run, or breathe the right way again. It all depended on his strength of will, and his therapy, but the signs were there: if he gave up and didn't do exactly what the doctors told him to, maintaining his position as a police officer in one of Boston's most prestigious departments would be difficult.

"You'll be back in no time," she assured him.

"How do you figure?" he asked.

"You used to be in a gang, right?"

"Maybe I still am," he mumbled.

"They gave you a hard time when you wanted to be a cop, right? But you did it anyway. You went against everything you knew and all your friends to do what you believed was right. That took a lot of guts. That same kind of courage is going to get you back on your feet and in the precinct in no time. I just know it."

He looked away.

"I wish I shared your enthusiasm," he mumbled.

"I brought you some flowers."

"What the fuck am I going to do with all these flowers?" he complained and glanced around at a room filled with roses and dandelions and sunflowers.

Avery leaned into his bed with a mischievous grin.

"I also brought you a bottle of whiskey," she whispered.

Finley's eyes lit up.

"Really?"

Avery pulled a bottle from under her jacket and slid it into the bed.

"You're going to be here for a while, right? You're a cop that typically lives on booze. What better motivator to get up and get your PT completed than some liquid fire?"

He went glassy at the sentiment.

"Thanks, Black. I appreciate that, really."

"You drew the fire away from me," she said. "That was really brave."

"Really *stupid*," he said and shook his head. "I've always been like that. Act first and think later. Fuckin' stupid. My mother always told me something like this would happen if I didn't calm down and think before I act."

Avery sat with him for a while. They hardly spoke. Finley had no desire to entertain and Avery had no desire to upset him.

"Fill me in," he eventually mumbled. "Anything new on the asshole?"

"Thompson and I went around to all the places where he was supposed to have worked or gone to class. They knew him. Everyone knew him. They said he was very gentle. Soft-spoken and kind. Never once got in an argument with anyone. Made me think of all those people you meet that seem happy on the outside, but on the inside they're really miserable, and you never know it until they commit suicide or ask for a divorce. He probably harbored a lot of anger and no one ever knew, and it just came out at the kill sites."

Finley shook his head.

"Fuckin' freaks."

*

At the A1, Avery walked through the first floor and headed to the offices in the back. A quick check of her watch revealed the time: one o'clock. *Punctual as always,* she thought.

Sloane Miller was excited to see her.

"Hello there," she said. "Come on in."

Avery sat on the couch and took a sip of coffee.

"How you doing?" Avery asked.

"I'm just fine," Sloane replied. "How are *you*?"

"I don't know," she said. "It's like we were talking about last week. Everything is going well. I'm having lunch with Rose today. The case is closed, a new case just opened, but I'm feeling a little anxious, and sad."

"That's normal," Sloane replied.

"How so?"

"Well, you just ended a major chapter in your life. You're onto a new chapter. While it's good to move on, sometimes we need to mourn the past, and mourn the person we were *in that moment.* That's often a slow process. It takes time."

"Yeah," Avery said. "That's how it feels. Like I want to cry all the time."

"Crying is good," she replied. "Gets things out. Let's us move on."

Avery nodded.

"Good," she said. "That's good to know."

They remained quiet. Avery could hear the tick of the clock in the room. Sloane had her hands in her lap and waited patiently for Avery to speak. When the silence went on for over five minutes, Sloane cleared her throat.

"Is there anything specific you want to work on today?" she asked. "It's nice to stay focused, and to use the time we have to target problem areas. An analogy I like to use is this: we open the box here, and then, when I'm not around, you can rummage around in the box all you want, and at least you know what needs to be seen. What needs to be seen, Avery?"

Ramirez was the first thought that came into her head.

"Relationships," she said. "I'm terrible with relationships. I keep screwing them up."

"Why do you do that?"

"They just never seem as important as work."

"Maybe they're not."

"What do you mean?"

"Maybe you need someone that lets you be who you are. Someone that doesn't mind you're always working. Someone that loves you for you."

The idea didn't feel right to Avery.

"No," she said. "I'm selfish. I know that now. I spent all my life running away from my past to get to some magical place where I could feel happy. First it was law. Then it was the police force. It's about time I stopped running and start to grow some roots. For that to happen, I know I need to give something up. I'm *ready* to give something up."

"Then maybe you just haven't found the person that you're willing to invest in, someone that makes you *want* to cut back on your hours at work or whatever it is you're willing to give up. Someone you *want* to change for."

Avery looked at her.

"Yeah," she said. "I think that's it."

"Is there someone you're thinking about?" Sloane wondered.

A smile came to Avery's face. She lowered her head and blushed.

"Maybe."

Avery imagined Ramirez sitting on his boat or alone at home. She wasn't sure where he might be or what he would say, but she was determined to make her feelings known.

"I've got someone I need to see," she said.

On the way out of the office, Avery was excited and scared at the same time. Her time would come for Ramirez.

But first it was time for her daughter.

She put in a call to Rose.

"Are we still on for lunch today?" she asked.

"Looking forward to it," Rose said. "Our usual place?"

Avery smiled wide, feeling a chance at her old life brewing again.

"Our usual place."

COMING SOON!

Book #3 in the Avery Black mystery series!

Blake Pierce

Blake Pierce is author of the bestselling RILEY PAGE mystery series, which include the mystery suspense thrillers ONCE GONE (book #1), ONCE TAKEN (book #2), ONCE CRAVED (#3), and ONCE LURED (#4). Blake Pierce is also the author of the MACKENZIE WHITE mystery series and the AVERY BLACK mystery series.

An avid reader and lifelong fan of the mystery and thriller genres, Blake loves to hear from you, so please feel free to visit www.blakepierceauthor.com to learn more and stay in touch.

BOOKS BY BLAKE PIERCE

RILEY PAIGE MYSTERY SERIES
ONCE GONE (Book #1)
ONCE TAKEN (Book #2)
ONCE CRAVED (Book #3)
ONCE LURED (Book #4)

MACKENZIE WHITE MYSTERY SERIES
BEFORE HE KILLS (Book #1)
BEFORE HE SEES (Book #2)

AVERY BLACK MYSTERY SERIES
CAUSE TO KILL (Book #1)
CAUSE TO RUN (Book #2)

CPSIA information can be obtained
at www.ICGtesting.com
Printed in the USA
FSOW03n2149300916
25617FS